Dog River Blues
By
Mike Jastrzebski

Mike Jastrzebski

Also by Mike Jastrzebski

Key Lime Blues (A Wes Darling Mystery)
The Storm Killer

Mike Jastrzebski

Special thanks to my wife, Mary, who is my first reader and constant editor. Thanks also to my critique group; Christine Kling, Neil Plakcy, Miriam Auerbach, Sharon Potts, and Christine Jackson.

Mike Jastrzebski

Chapter 1

The last time I saw Elvis, not *the* Elvis, mind you, he was sitting on the dock in Key West waiting to see me off. He'd had one of his dreams, and although he knew I was a skeptic, he felt it was his duty to bring me the news. "Wes, your grandfather's dead."

It was a cool, sunny, February day and I was stowing gear, preparing to take my sailboat, *Rough Draft*, over to the Bahamas for a couple of months before the hurricane season hit. I thought I'd misheard him. I stopped what I was doing and stepped off the boat and onto the dock.

Elvis was a couple of inches taller than me, and much thinner. His head was shaved and polished, and he had a Van Dyke style beard. Elvis wore a dark blue pinstriped suit, and white gloves.

He'd brought along a small cooler filled with beer and was sitting next to it on a blanket with his feet hanging over the side of the dock. As I helped myself to a Miller Lite Elvis took off his jacket, folded it with exaggerated care, and set it on the blanket. He moved it an inch to the right, two inches to the left, a smidgeon up, until it was in just the proper place to satisfy his sensibilities. Obsessive

Compulsive Disorder will do that to a person. I popped the cap on my beer and sat down next to him.

"Your dream's a little old," I said. "My grandfather died seven years ago. The big 'C'. He smoked all his life."

Elvis was watching a pelican, a big bird with the grace of a slapstick comic, and the eyesight of a dive-bomber. As the bird hit the water with an awkward splash, Elvis turned his attention to me. "Not that grandfather. Your father's father."

According to my mother, I was a result of a wild weekend in Acapulco with a Vietnam vet she met at a club. I didn't know my father's name. I didn't know where he was from. I didn't even know if he was alive or dead. At this stage in my life I didn't really care.

"Never knew him," I said. "Or anyone else on that side of the family."

"Maybe it's time," Elvis said.

"For what?"

"To get to know your family."

I looked at Elvis, but he was staring down at the water, avoiding my gaze. "You know I don't believe in that psychic shit, or ghosts and UFOs for that matter."

"I thought that after what happened last month, you'd believe me."

He was referring to a nighttime visit he'd had from the ghost of Celine Stewart, a girl whose death convinced me I no longer wanted to be a P.I. I wasn't ready to admit that I believed he had real psychic abilities, or that he'd spoken to Celine's ghost, but the information he provided did aid the police in locating her body.

"Elvis, you and I both know there's no such thing as psychics."

"How do you explain Celine?" he asked.

"You offered to hire me," I reminded him. "I suspect you have other detectives working for you. One of your investigators must have stumbled upon something the cops missed."

Elvis turned to me. "I don't have any investigators working for me. No bullshit, Wes. I spoke with your grandfather."

I set my empty bottle next to Elvis and jumped up. "I don't have time for this, Elvis. I'm going to the Bahamas."

"He said you need to go to Mobile."

"Alabama?"

Elvis got to his feet. "He says he can't rest until the book is found and returned to its rightful owner."

"I'm not a librarian."

Elvis shrugged. "I'm just the messenger."

"What book?" I asked, regretting it as soon as the words left my mouth.

"He didn't say."

"Of course not. And who is the rightful owner—wait, let me guess, he didn't say."

Elvis shrugged. "I don't choose who visits my dreams, and I don't ask them questions. They tell me what they want me to know."

"Why me?"

"You're a detective."

"Was a detective," I reminded him. Elvis knew I used to work for my family's detective agency. He also knew I hated the work.

DDA Security was founded in 1876 by my great-great-great-grandfather, Aaron 'Dusty' Darling. Dusty had been a Pinkerton detective, a Wells Fargo shotgun driver, and he even knew Wyatt Earp and Doc Holliday. When he was forty-five he left the Wild West, moved to Detroit, and started the firm. Back then it was called The Darling Detective Agency. Now my mother ran the agency and my quitting was a major bone of contention between us.

"Your grandfather thinks you can help."

"I can't. I'm not a detective anymore."

"Like I said, Wes. I'm just the messenger."

I swore and spun away from Elvis and climbed back on board *Rough Draft*.

When I was young, I'd dreamed of meeting my father. For years I begged my mother for information. She'd always denied knowing anything about him other than that he was a Vietnam vet and that they'd spent one wonderful weekend together in Mexico. She refused to tell me his name.

Somewhere in my middle teens I'd come to accept the fact that I was never going to know my father. Eventually it stopped mattering. At least that's what I told myself as I picked up the phone and called my mother.

"Yes," she admitted when I wouldn't let the subject rest. "Your father was from Mobile."

"Is he alive?" I asked.

"I don't know."

"What about the rest of his family?" I asked.

"I don't know anything about them."

I didn't believe her, but I knew my mother well enough to know I wasn't going to get anything else from her. If I wanted to know about my father or his side of my family, I was going to have to find out for myself. I hung up the phone, plotted a new course, and finished preparing to leave Key West.

***

Ten days later I was docked at a small marina on the Dog River in Mobile, Alabama. I'd just finished eating breakfast and was sitting in the cockpit drinking coffee when I noticed a tall, dark-haired woman strolling along the dock toward me. She wore faded jeans and a short blue top that showed an occasional flash of skin. To my surprise, when she reached my boat she stopped.

"You Wes Darling?"

When I nodded she shook off her sandals and stepped, uninvited, onto my boat.

"I'm your cousin Jessica Wolfe." She sat opposite me and pointed to my coffee cup. "Got any more of that?"

"It's customary to wait until you're invited before you step onto someone's boat."

"Sorry," she said without meaning it. "We gotta talk, you and me. Family matters."

I'd grown a beard since leaving Key West, and I wasn't sure if I liked it or not. I found myself pulling at it with my fingers while I studied her. I didn't know what to make of this brash woman who had wandered into my life. Wasn't sure I wanted her on my boat. Short of tossing her overboard, I wasn't sure what to do about getting her to leave.

"What makes you think I'm interested in family matters?"

"I heard you been asking around about us."

"I recently learned my father was from around here. Just because I'm curious doesn't mean I want to get involved."

She leaned forward and I caught a whiff of jasmine. "You here about the book?"

I groaned and looked out across the water. I did not want to admit to Elvis that he'd been right—again.

"What book?" I asked.

"When Granddaddy came home from World War Two he brought back a book he took off a dead German soldier. Before he died he told Gran he wanted her to see that it got back to the people it belongs to."

"How'd you know where to find me?" I asked.

"Your mother called. Took Gran by surprise. She told me she hadn't heard from your mother in close to twenty years. Didn't know when you'd get here of course, but it didn't take me long to find you after you started asking around about the family."

I stood, picked up my cup and climbed down into the cabin. It was all I could do to keep from throwing my cup against one of the bulkheads. My mother had admitted to me that my father was from Mobile but claimed she didn't know anything else about the family. Now I discover she'd been in contact with my grandparents.

I took a deep breath, held it for ten seconds, and then dragged out a cup for Jessica. I filled it without asking how she liked her coffee and topped mine off before rejoining her in the cockpit.

I handed her the cup and sat down across from her. "Tell me about this book."

"Do you know what an illuminated manuscript is?" she asked.

"Some kind of handwritten book, I think?"

"More than that. I did a little research on the web after Granddaddy died. They go back to the Egyptians and were the only source of books until the printing press was invented. They were done for royalty or the clergy. Some of them are worth millions. Far as I can tell, this one dates from the Renaissance period, thirteen or fourteen hundred A.D. maybe. It's what they call a book of hours, a prayer book of sorts from what I understand. This one has some pretty fancy artwork. Granddaddy kept it in a special case in his office. Didn't let many people see it. He was afraid someone would want to know where he got it."

I hated to admit it; my curiosity was piqued.

"And where's the book now?" I asked.

"It was stolen. I was kind of hoping you could help me find it."

"Why me? Isn't there anyone else who can look for the book?"

She shifted her body so that she could look out across the river to the marshy grasslands that bordered the marina. I followed her gaze and watched a large gator slide into the water. The boat rocked as a lingering breeze brushed the water into soft chocolate ribbons and nibbled at her hair. The air smelled of salt water, gasoline, burning leaves, and jasmine.

"I don't know who else to turn to. Uncle Roy, he's kind of crazy. Has been since he came back from the army in seventy-five. Least that's what Daddy tells me. I'm afraid he might kill someone. I wouldn't want that.

"Daddy tried to do something," Jessica added. "He went to see Sam Quinlin, the lawyer we hired to look into finding the rightful owner."

My mind was awhirl, and not just because I was trying to digest the information Jessica had provided. Since Jessica had referred to me as her cousin, that meant her father was my uncle. But what about this Uncle Roy? Was he my father? Curiosity had brought me to Mobile, but was I really ready to find out? After all, he hadn't even tried to contact me in over thirty years. Did I dare ask her?

"Are you listening to me, Wes?" Jessica's voice intruded into my thoughts.

"Sorry," I said. "I was distracted. Did you go to the police?"

"Granddaddy didn't come by the book legally. We all thought it would be better if we kept the police out of it.

"The night after he talked to the lawyer, Daddy was beat near to death. That's the night the manuscript was stolen."

"So even after someone steals the book and beats up your dad, you didn't go to the police?"

"Nope." Jessica took a sip of her coffee and made a face. "Who taught you how to make coffee?"

"I like my coffee. And I don't see how I can help you find the manuscript."

Jessica shrugged; a sensual movement that made me wish we weren't related. Her face was delicately shaped and pale. It was as if it had been sculpted from fine marble. Even her mouth had an artistic, chiseled look about it. But her eyes told the real story. They were blue and fierce, and I could tell by the way she met my gaze that she wasn't going to take no for an answer.

"All I want you to do is go talk to the lawyer we hired. Sam was going to make some calls to someone he knew in the State Department and see if he could find out who the manuscript belonged to and how we could return it. Next thing we know the book's stolen. Gran wants to just let it go, but I want to do what Granddaddy asked."

"If I help you find the book how do I know you won't just sell it and keep the money? You claim to be my cousin, but I don't know you from Adam."

Jessica's body stiffened and for the first time in my life I understood the meaning of the phrase, *If looks could kill.* I held up my hands in apology before she could take a swing at me. "Sorry, I'll take you at your word." For the time being, I thought, as she continued on.

"Way I figure it, the lawyer has to know something. He won't take our calls. Besides, no one else knew about this except family."

"The lawyer beat up your dad?"

She gave her head an almost imperceptible shake. "Not exactly."

Talking to this girl was like pulling teeth from a rabid dog. I sighed, picked up our cups, and nodded toward the cabin. "I'll make us another pot," I said. "You want to come in?"

"I'll wait out here."

"That's fine," I said. "But when I come out I want some answers."

As I made a fresh pot of coffee, I gave some thought to her story. She was obviously holding something back from me.

My mother's father once gave me an important piece of advice: "Whoever speaks first loses." It was something that had helped me more than once in the past. This time when I sat opposite Jessica I set our cups down, folded my arms, looked her dead in the eye, and didn't say a word.

"What?" she asked.

"You seem to be avoiding the subject of who beat up your dad."

"Avoiding is a strong word."

"So who the hell beat him up?"

"Fish Conners."

"What kind of a person goes by the name Fish?" I asked.

Jessica sipped her coffee. A breeze passed over her, and her scent made my nose quiver. "Fish got his name when he was younger. He used to fish a lot. When he was a teenager they said he could drink like a fish. The name stuck."

A pelican made a clownish dive into the river and I shook my head. "You're a colorful lot down here, aren't you?"

"Despite what you northerners seem to think, we're not all rednecks."

"I never thought that," I said. "But there have already been a couple of times when I was talking to one of the locals and felt like I needed an interpreter."

Jessica grinned. "I gotta admit, I was gonna lie to you, cousin. The truth is—Fish is just mean. He never got over the fact that he blew out a knee and got cut from the University of Alabama football team. He's big and he's fast, and he'll do anything for a buck. He's gotta be working for someone."

"Which takes us back to the lawyer," I said.

"Sam Quinlin."

"And you want me to what? Politely ask him if he stole the book? And if he did, please return it."

"There you go." She jumped up and drew a folded piece of paper from her pocket. "Here's my number and Sam Quinlin's office address. Either way you decide let me know." Not waiting for my reply, she climbed out of the boat and headed down the dock.

"I really don't want to get involved," I called out after her.

She glanced over her shoulder. "Think about it, then give me a call. Don't wait too long though. If you aren't going to help, I got to find someone else. By the way, how old are you, Wes, thirty-four, thirty-five?"

"Close," I said. "Why do you ask?"

"Just wondering how a person your age can afford to buy a sailboat and travel around without working, that's all."

"Where I come from we don't ask those kinds of questions."

"If you don't want to answer, that's okay. But I got a lot more questions for you, cousin." She turned away and sashayed down the dock, a young woman who moved to the beat of no drummer I'd ever heard before.

I was wondering whether I should run after her and ask her about my father, when she turned the corner and disappeared behind the marina store. As for her story, I wasn't sure what to believe. I also wasn't buying her country-girl act. I got the feeling she was a little more sophisticated than what she wanted me to believe.

Chapter 2

That evening I wandered down to the gathering area. Most marinas have one. At one place I visited it was the office where chairs lined the walls and a table sat in the middle of the room with a perpetual jigsaw puzzle under construction. At another it was a screened-in porch. At the Bay View Marina it was a large, round, outdoor table set under a recent addition to the restaurant which was built on large wooden pilings. It overlooked the river, was lighted, and had a ceiling fan that helped chase away the no-see-ums and mosquitoes.

I found Rusty Dawson sitting alone at the table tossing down a Budweiser. A dour-looking man in his sixties, Rusty's silver hair still showed an occasional red highlight. His eyes were alert, despite the six empty beer cans lined up along the edge of the table.

I'd met Rusty the previous afternoon. When I pulled in he was sitting on a bench in front of the marina store staring out across the river. As I swung the boat around and headed for the dock he walked over, grabbed my line and expertly tied me off to a piling.

"Hey, buddy, how you doing?" Rusty said when he saw me. Reaching into the small cooler at his side, he

19

pulled out a beer and tossed it to me. "Take a load off, why don't you."

I sat down and popped the lid on my beer. "Funny thing happened today, Rusty. I got a visit from a woman who claims to be my cousin Jessica."

Rusty turned his head and spit out of the corner of his mouth. "You got family around here?"

"So it seems. I found out my father was from the area."

"What's his last name?"

"Wolfe," I said.

"There's been Wolfe's around here nigh onto a hundred and fifty years." Rusty sat back in his chair, rested his hands on his belly and looked up at the ceiling fan. "You get this girl's daddy's name?"

I shook my head. "No, but she mentioned an Uncle Roy."

"That would be John and Fran's son."

"So you know the family?"

"Never much liked John. He was a real son-of-a-bitch. I think John and Fran have a granddaughter named Jessica."

I finished my beer and he shoved another across the table. After popping the top I folded my hands around the can and leaned back into my chair. I suspected that if I asked about my father, Rusty would be able to answer at least the basic questions of who, what, and where he was. I wasn't sure I was ready to learn the answers to those questions.

Instead, I asked, "Rusty, you know a guy by the name of Fish Conners?"

He raised an eyebrow and took a good swig of his beer. "He's meaner than a hungry gator. What business you got with him?"

"Not me. It seems this Conners fellow had a run-in with my uncle."

"That's too bad. I guess I would a heard if Fish killed him."

"Is he capable of killing someone?"

"He's a big man with a short fuse. I never heard that he killed anyone, but that doesn't mean anything. Fish is a bayou boy. For all I know Fish could've killed a dozen people. Sometimes a body will turn up along these waterways. After the gators get hold of 'em there ain't no way to know how they died."

I thought about the large alligator I'd seen sunning itself on the bank of the Dog River that morning. I tried not to think about the kind of damage a creature like that could do to a man as I mulled over the implications.

"Let me lay one more name on you, Rusty. You know anything about a lawyer name of Sam Quinlin?"

Rusty cleared his throat and spit to the side again. "Don't recognize that name. You've been in town what, little over a day? What do you need a lawyer for?"

"Not for me," I said. "The family hired him to look into some legal matters about some book my grandfather brought back from Europe after the war. The book was stolen and Jessica thinks Quinlin might have hired Fish Conners to steal it. She wanted me to check into it."

"Why you?"

"I used to be a PI. I think Jessica got it in her head that I could help."

Rusty stared over my shoulder at the river. With a sigh he pushed himself away from the table and stood.

"I left my cell on the boat. I think I know someone I can call." He turned and walked off toward the docks that ran behind the restaurant without waiting for my thanks. He moved with sure steps and I was left with the impression of a young man wandering about in an old man's body. I wondered how he managed it. I counted the cans lined up on the table. They now numbered eight.

While I waited, I finished my beer and then swiveled my chair around so that it faced the river. A lone shrimp boat had just come in from the bay and was headed up Dog River. A long line of gulls and pelicans trailed behind it looking for handouts as the crew culled the day's take. Several more pelicans glided in from the north like prehistoric pterodactyls, and then dove on the boat.

I jumped when Rusty walked up behind me and spoke. "Have another beer if you'd like." I swung my chair back around and reached into the cooler.

Rusty took his seat across from me and grabbed the last beer. "Sam Quinlin has a small office off Government Street. It's a one-man operation; doesn't even have a full time receptionist. Just some girl who comes in twice a week to do filing."

"I wonder why the family chose him."

"I asked why someone might hire Quinlin. Seems he's been running late night ads on TV. Offers low rates, walk-ins welcome. Here, you'll need this." Rusty held out a piece of paper, and when I took it from him I noticed it was a crude map with an address and a phone number on it.

I nodded toward the marina store off to our right. "How about if I get the next six-pack?"

"Appreciate that, partner." Rusty spit, stood and gulped down the rest of his beer. "But I've got something I've got to take care of right now. I'll take a rain check though."

Rusty shoved the empty cans into his cooler, nodded, and headed toward the parking lot. He stopped at the trash bin, dumped the contents of the cooler, and walked over to a burgundy, twenty-year-old tank of a Cadillac. The car was in cherry condition and looked like it had just been driven off the showroom floor.

As he pulled out of the lot I crumbled up the paper Rusty had given me and tucked it into my pocket to be thrown away later. I was a stranger to the area and I'd pretty much decided that I couldn't offer much help in finding the stolen book. What the hell did I know about good old boys and bayous? For that matter, I didn't much care if they found the old book or not. Confident in my decision, I headed upstairs to the restaurant.

A short, heavyset girl with big hair and too many tattoos was seated at a table drinking coffee and wrapping silverware in cloth napkins. When she saw me she pushed herself away from the table, grabbed a menu, and waddled over. I looked around and saw that there were only about a half dozen people seated around the restaurant. Two more sat at the bar. "Can I eat at the bar?"

The waitress shrugged as if she was too busy to care and held out the menu to me. "Cathy'll take your order."

Cathy turned out to be a leggy blonde woman of about thirty. She was standing behind the bar in her bare feet, all five-foot-ten of her. As I sat down she walked over to where a young wiry guy with a military style haircut was sitting. He looked like he was about to fall off his stool.

"You've had enough, Billy," she said. "Go home."

Billy started to argue, but a man in his mid-forties, with bulging shoulders and arm muscles, slid off his own stool and moved over next to the boy. He clapped a massive hand on Billy's shoulder and said, "Come on Billy. I'll walk you down to the boat. I'm sure Lizbeth's worried about you."

Billy tried to pull away, but the older man's hand stayed put and he helped Billy off the seat and guided him toward the door. As they left I turned to Cathy. "I used to bartend down in Key West. More often than not when a friend steps in like that the person he's trying to help takes offense, might even throw a swing. The older guy was taking a chance."

She looked at me for the first time and her dark cloudy eyes lit up. When she smiled my stomach did a little shuffle.

"Billy's harmless enough. And as for Jack, I wouldn't let him hear you refer to him as the older guy. Then there would be a fight. I'm Cathy by the way. What'll you have?"

"Wes." I placed my order for a burger and a Miller Lite. When she set my beer in front of me I tilted the bottle in her direction, a silent acknowledgement of her advice.

As I ate my burger, I watched Cathy work. She had long delicate fingers and moved with smooth easy motions as she twisted and turned and bent over to pick something up from the floor. I wouldn't describe her as beautiful. Her ears were a shade too large, her cheeks a little too sculpted, but I couldn't take my eyes off her.

In between serving the occasional customer she drifted over to where I sat and we chatted.

"Sounds like you're from the Midwest," she said at one point.

"Michigan."

"Then we were practically neighbors. I was born and raised in Wisconsin."

I mentioned that I brought my sailboat in the previous day and that I had some family in the area. She told me she'd accidentally stopped in Mobile, and it suited her. She'd bought a small houseboat and was living aboard in the marina.

We volleyed back and forth and as I was getting up to leave I asked, "How about going out to a movie and dinner with me?"

She frowned, and just when I thought she was going to shoot me down she turned her smile back on. "You like the blues, Wes?"

"I enjoy listening to good blues music, if that's what you mean."

"Tomorrow night is free mudbug night at the Blues Cafe. It won't cost a lot of money and you might have a little fun while you're at it."

"What's a mudbug?" I asked.

"Crawfish, honey. Spicy and hot. You game?"

"I'll try anything once."

"Good." She spun around, stopped, and looked at me over her shoulder. "I know you just pulled in and don't have a car, so I'll drive. Meet you out front at five-thirty tomorrow."

I finished my beer, left a twenty on the counter, and headed outside. I tripped and almost fell on my ass trying to navigate the wooden steps that led downstairs, and making my way along the dock was more of a chore than it should have been. I realized that I was a bit drunk. I'd downed three Buds when I was talking to Rusty and another three beers while I sat in the bar.

A sport fishing boat was docked a little way down from *Rough Draft*, and as I walked by I sensed movement. I started to turn, stumbled, and fell to one knee. As I looked over my shoulder a dark shape swished past my head so close that I felt my hair lift in the wind.

Without thinking I dropped my shoulder and rolled forward. Out of the corner of my eye I watched a fishing gaff slam against the wood piling to my left, ringing out with a dull metallic thud.

Somewhere in the distant reaches of my mind an anxious voice urged me to get my ass in gear. Before I could move, a boot came out of nowhere and caught me in the ribs. I cried out, and at my inner voice's command, I tried to scramble to my knees as another kick tore into my right shoulder. My jacket did little to blunt the force of the attack. I was getting the shit beat out of me and I was too drunk to respond. In my altered state, I saw only one avenue of escape. Before my attacker could pummel me again, I curled my body into a ball and rolled into the Dog River.

The plunge into the icy water did a lot to sober me up. My first thought as I kicked off the muddy bottom of the river was that someone was trying to kill me. My second was why? I've often been accused of having a knack for pissing off people, but I'd only been at the marina for a little over twenty-four hours and met maybe six people. That was a record even for me.

As I broke the surface I sucked in a mouthful of cool clear air and let myself sink back under the surface. My attacker was still on the dock and he swung the gaff toward me. It splashed over my head and came down through the water with enough force to do some serious damage had it hit me.

I cursed to myself and let the current and the ebb tide tug me away from the dock. Cold wrapped its icy fingers around me. My jacket and shoes dragged me down toward the muddy bottom of the river, and I couldn't shake the vision from my mind of that eight foot alligator I'd spotted across from the marina.

I kicked off my shoes, peeled off my jacket and swam back to the surface. This time I was far enough from the dock that my attacker couldn't reach me. "Hey," I heard someone call out from the other end of the dock. "What's going on down there?"

My attacker, a large shadow with hidden features, looked from me to the man who had called out and back to me. I was shivering and could barely manage to dog paddle parallel to the dock, away from my enemy. I was weakening and I wondered how the hell I'd get out of the water even if I could reach the dock.

"Hey, I need some help out here," the same voice called out.

The shadow on the dock took three long steps and jumped into the sport fishing boat. I listened to the engine grind, and then catch. It only took a moment for me to realize that the prop was far more likely to chew me up than the gator I'd seen earlier.

Changing direction, I found some hidden source of energy I didn't know I had. I was almost to the safety of the dock when the boat lurched forward. The hull slammed into me, tossed me aside, and battered me against a wood piling. The wake rose up as the boat sped away and smashed my head into something solid. The night darkened and I began the long slide into the void.

With oblivion comes deliverance. God reached down and drew me upward, and the next thing I knew I was coughing up a lungful of water onto the dock and looking into the salty face of the man Cathy had called Jack, who'd helped the young drunk home from the bar earlier. Another man was pacing back and forth on the dock behind him.

When I tried to sit up the second man got down on his knees and put a hand on my chest. "Just lay there for a couple of minutes." When I complied he took off his jacket and placed it over me. For the first time I noticed that he wore a priest's collar.

"I was heading to my boat when I heard someone call for help," Jack said. "That must have been you, Father." The priest nodded and Jack went on. "There was a guy standing on the dock looking down into the water and at first I thought it was him that called. I figured you fell in and he was trying to drag you out, but when I started running down the dock, the son of a bitch jumped into the boat and took off. Tell you the truth, I thought you were dead. You all right?"

"My right shoulder and arm feels like it's been sliced and diced."

The priest moved his face in close to take a look.

"The barnacles on the piling cut you up. There's a lot of blood, but it doesn't look too bad. Can't be sure in this light though."

"Any idea who attacked you?" Jack asked.

"Not a clue," I said.

"He looked like someone I've seen around," the priest said. "His name's Fish Conners, but I couldn't swear it was him. I was too far away to see his face."

"So how the hell'd you drag me out of the water?"

"That wasn't me," the priest said. I looked over at Jack and he smiled.

"Been hauling shrimp most of my life. Good thing it's high tide. I just grabbed your belt and heaved. We'd better call the cops, huh. That asshole tried to kill you."

"Did you recognize the guy?" I asked.

He shook his head.

"You didn't happen to get a boat name or registration number, did you?"

"I was too busy trying to find you and pull you out of the water."

I turned my gaze back to the priest. "You can't swear it was Fish Conners?"

"Not with any confidence."

"Then there's not much reason to call the cops," I said.

The two men stood and the shrimper grabbed my hand and levered me to my feet. I was shivering so hard that the priest's jacket slipped from my hands and fell to the dock. My teeth began to chatter and my shoulder felt as if someone had placed a layer of hot charcoal briquettes under the skin.

The priest snatched up the jacket and threw it over my shoulders. "We need to get you someplace warm."

"I'll let you take care of him from here, Father," Jack said, as he turned and started walking down the dock.

"Thanks again," I called out.

The priest put a hand on my arm and gave it a little tug. "Come on, Wes. Let's get you inside your boat so you can warm up."

I stopped and pulled away from the priest. I was no longer drunk and my mind was working just fine, despite the fact that my body was shaking so badly my words came out in a stutter. "Who are you and how the hell do you know my name?"

"I'm your Uncle Ben. I was on my way down here to talk to you when I saw you being attacked."

Chapter 3

B en, I was having trouble thinking of him as Uncle Ben or Father Ben, helped me over to *Rough Draft*. I had a monster headache and I felt like I'd taken a spill off a trampoline. I almost passed out as I stepped down into the cockpit and would have fallen if he hadn't steadied me.

"Could you grab the flashlight?" I pointed to the storage cubby above the starboard seat. When Ben turned it on, I slid out the washboards, and snapped the flexible plastic door in place.

I grabbed a handhold, made my way down the steps, and switched on the light before turning to face the priest. "You want to come in?"

"Someone needs to clean that shoulder for you. It's still bleeding."

I was about to argue the point when a wave of nausea washed over me. I barely made it to the settee.

"You got a first aid kit?" Ben asked.

"In the head. Right hand door above the toilet."

I closed my eyes and lay back on the settee and must have passed out. The next thing I knew Ben was shaking me and saying something. His face looked grim.

"What?" I asked.

"Your shoulder looks like raw meat. On top of that, you've got some slivers in there and maybe some broken pieces of barnacle. It's going to hurt like hell when I clean it out."

Ben had cut the sleeve off my shirt while I'd been out and when I moved my shoulder a blast of pain ran up and down my arm. A flock of black spots floated before my eyes and I would have slid back down into the settee if Ben hadn't grabbed me.

"Maybe we should get you to the hospital," he said.

"Go ahead and clean the arm," I said. "I've been banged up worse than this before."

"It's your call. I'll need a couple of clean towels."

I directed him to the locker under the front berth and while he went for the towels I took a moment to wonder what the hell was going on. If Ben was right and my attacker was Fish Conners, then someone had told Fish about me. There were only two people who knew that I was considering helping out the family. Jessica and Rusty. And then there was the timing of Ben's appearance. It was time for some answers.

"How did you happen to be here, Ben? I mean, eleven o'clock is kind of late for a casual visit."

Ben laid a towel across my lap, opened the first aid kit, and took out a pair of tweezers. He took my wrist in his left hand and gently turned my shoulder toward the light, then he attacked my arm with the tweezers.

"Jessica asked me to stop by and talk to you," he said.

I closed my eyes against the sharp biting pain and when I opened them he was holding a two inch sliver of wood up for my inspection.

"This is the biggest one." He placed it on the open towel and met my gaze. "Why don't you let me fix up this arm first, then I'll answer any questions you have. I don't think you want me talking and probing at the same time."

I nodded and gritted my teeth as he went back to work. Fifteen minutes later he set the tweezers down next to the mounting pile of slivers and broken shells and reached for the bottle of peroxide.

I bit my lip and tasted blood when Ben poured the peroxide over my shoulder. Leaning back into the cushion I closed my eyes as he dabbed the shoulder dry. He finished up wrapping my arm in gauze, and then he sat on the settee across from me.

"Can I get you anything?" he asked.

I shook my head no and the movement made me feel like I was going to pass out again.

"Maybe I should leave and let you get some rest." Ben stood. "I can come back tomorrow."

"I want to know why you're here," I said.

"I was visiting with a sick parishioner. On the way home I decided to stop and see if you were still up." Ben carried the bloodied towels over to the sink and began rinsing them. "Jessica thought you might have some questions about the family. She didn't feel comfortable talking to you about the dynamics of our family."

"Do I understand this right? You're Jessica's father? I thought priests couldn't be married or have children."

Ben wrung out the towels and set them alongside the sink. "I came to my vocation late in life. My wife died when Jessica was three. I began my studies after Jessica started college. I've only been a priest for a year now. But I didn't really come here to talk about me."

"So you came to convince me to help find the book?"

Ben moved back to the seat across from me. He rested his elbows on his knees and leaned toward me. He caught my eyes with his and smiled a friendly smile. He looked just like I'd expect a priest to look, but the words that came out of his mouth were anything but priest-like.

"I don't give a damn about that book. As far as I'm concerned, my father's going to roast in hell for eternity whether the book's returned to its rightful owner or not. Whoever stole that book stole it from a thief, who stole it from a thief."

"Tough language for a priest."

Ben's smile turned to a sheepish grin. "Some habits die hard. I owned my own construction business for most of my life. The language goes with the business."

"So if it's not the book, why are you here?"

"Jessica never knew James. She thought I should be the one to talk to you."

"So my father, you said his name was James, he's what, dead?"

"We don't know. Father threw James out of the house a week after he turned sixteen. Nobody's heard from him since then. Your Uncle Roy hired a P.I. to search for him a couple of years ago. No luck."

The information hit me like I'd been kicked in the gut by a mule. I felt queasy all over again and I had to take several deep breaths before I could speak.

"So why was he kicked out? Drugs?"

Ben leaned back into the settee, steepled his fingers, and rested his hands on his chest. He appeared to be choosing his words carefully.

"James smoked a little pot once in awhile, who didn't back then. But the truth is our father was a grade 'A' prick." There was another pause, a little more contemplation, and then he continued. "Father was a Baptist minister and James was a pugnacious kid. You know how teens are. They question everything. The two of them got into an argument. James challenged Father's beliefs. Told him he didn't believe there was a God. Father told him he could not believe someplace else.

"Mother was always kind to us, but she was submissive to her husband. She recently told me that not standing up for James was her biggest regret in life."

"How did your father react to you becoming a priest?"

"About how you'd expect from a man like him. As far as he was concerned I didn't exist any longer. He never spoke another word to me after I told him I was going to a Catholic seminary. It's not surprising, really. He stopped speaking to Roy after he got out of the army. Roy dared to express his opinion that the government had made a mistake fighting the Viet Nam War. To Father it was always God and country first. Never family."

"So why the urgent need to get back the book?"

"I told you. I don't care about the book. This is Jessica's project. She's the only one Father cared about. She was his little angel. As far as she was concerned, he could do no harm. He said something to her about wanting to find the owner of the book and return it. That's been her mission since he died."

"And yet you went up against Fish Conners and took a beating trying to get it back."

Ben looked confused. "Whatever gave you that idea? I've never met Fish Conners in my life. I've seen him around; he grew up not far from here. That's why I couldn't swear it was him that attacked you. It was dark and I didn't get a good enough view of his face."

"Jessica told me the reason she needed my help getting the book back was that Fish beat you up when you went to see Sam Quinlin about the manuscript."

Another blank look. "Who's Sam Quinlin?"

"The lawyer the family hired to find the rightful owner of the book," I said.

Ben shook his head. "I'm lost here, Wes. My mother mentioned she was hiring a lawyer, but she never told me who it was. And what does all of this have to do with Fish Conners?"

"I don't know," I said.

I thought about what Ben had said and wondered who was lying to me, Ben or Jessica. Being a priest didn't guarantee he wouldn't lie to me. I was not a happy camper. Pushing myself up from the settee I groaned as the pain washed over me. I must have looked bad because Ben jumped up and reached out to support me.

"I still think you should let me drive you to the hospital," he said.

I shook his arm off. "I'll be fine. I'll take some aspirin and get to bed as soon as you leave."

Ben took the hint and headed for the steps. I had one last question for him before he left.

"If it was Fish who attacked me, who do you think told him I was interested in the book? The only two people who knew that were Jessica and Rusty Dawson."

Ben raised an eyebrow. "Rusty's an old friend of Mother's. How do you know him?"

"He keeps a boat here at the marina. Seems to hang around a lot, drinking and telling stories."

"It doesn't surprise me. Rusty's had some bad breaks. His wife died of cancer not long ago. And if I remember right, a couple of years ago his son was arrested for selling drugs. He might still be in prison."

"Rusty said he knew Fish," I said.

"Then he probably told Fish about you. Like you said, he likes to drink and tell stories. Hell, when I was a kid he'd come to visit and tell us kids about his life as a spy."

"He doesn't strike me as a spy type."

Ben shrugged. "He's an old man now. Drinks too much. Back then he had an aura about him. Maybe I just wanted to believe I knew a spy."

I hesitated to suggest what was on my mind, but the question had to be asked. "Do you think Jessica might have told Fish I was looking for the book?"

"Why would she do that?" he asked.

"Maybe she figured that if Fish came after me I'd be more likely to help her."

Ben seemed to mull the idea over for a few moments. "Jessica's always been a determined girl—actually I guess she's a woman now. I'd hate to think she set you up for a beating, but...."

I interrupted him. "But she might."

"I hope not." He turned and started up the steps. When he reached the cockpit he looked back at me. "Don't be too hard on her. She's just trying to do what your grandfather asked of her."

Chapter 4

I t was noon by the time I crawled out of bed. My shoulder felt as if an army of fire ants had built a nest under the skin and my head throbbed to a funky beat that threatened to drive me insane.

To make matters worse, as I stepped buck-naked into the main cabin I found my cousin peeking down at me through the clear plastic door that separated the cockpit from the interior of the boat. With a startled curse I did a backward jig and slid into the head.

Retrieving the still damp shorts I'd worn the night before when I went for my unexpected swim, I pulled them on and stomped back out into the cabin.

"I live alone on a boat because I like my privacy." I joined her in the cockpit, shivering as the cool air washed over me. It smelled of saw-grass and muck and diesel fuel.

Jessica jumped to her feet and reached out and took my hand. She held it, twisting it gently as she moved in close to me and examined my arm. "Daddy said you got hurt."

Her fingers lingered and I felt my knees weaken as she looked anxiously up into my face.

"You can't just walk onto someone's boat witho
being invited." I tried to sound stern, but I felt my anger
dissipating.

"You didn't call." She was pouting now and she
pushed my hand away. "And I needed to make sure you
were all right."

"I'm fine." I pointed off toward the marina store and
tried to keep my voice gruff. "You can go down and have a
seat at the table under the restaurant while I change into
something a little warmer."

"Why don't I just wait here for you? There's nothing I
haven't already seen, Darling."

I blushed at the thought of having been caught with
my pants down, and at the double entendre I detected in
her voice when Jessica used my last name. "I said I'll meet
you down by the restaurant."

I expected an argument, but Jessica just shrugged and
climbed off the boat. "Don't keep me waiting too long,
okay Cuz?" she said, as she walked away.

Despite Jessica's request not to keep her waiting, I
took my time changing and stopped at the marina store on
my way to meet her. I picked up two cups of coffee and
the last three donuts they had. I considered my options as
I waited for Jean, the girl who ran the store, to ring me up.

My first inclination was to tell Jessica to get lost, but if
it was Fish Conners who attacked me, it looked like I was
going to be dragged into this affair whether I liked it or
not.

Then there was my cousin. The girl set my blood to
boiling and left me slightly confused when she was around.

sin she was forbidden fruit, although I found
as hell and flirtatious to boot.

t getting ready to leave," Jessica said.

I set down the coffee and offered her a donut. She grabbed the chocolate covered cruller and left me with the two cinnamon donuts. One more reason to tell her I wasn't going to help.

"You're the one who's asking for help," I pointed out.

"About that." She took a bite out of the donut that left a smear of chocolate above her lip. Using the back of her hand she wiped it away and took another bite. "I thought we could drive out and see Sam Quinlin about the book."

I looked at my watch and shook my head. "I need to change the oil on *Rough Draft* this afternoon, and I've got plans this evening." When I saw the look of disappointment flash across her face I added, "I'll go with you tomorrow if you'd like."

"You've only been here two days, Wes. Don't tell me you have a date."

When I nodded she threw the last bite of the donut down next to her untouched coffee cup. "Around here, family comes before everything else."

I broke one of the donuts in two and dunked the smallest piece in my coffee cup. "Two weeks ago I didn't even know you existed."

"Doesn't matter. We're still family."

"Which is why I agreed to go with you tomorrow. Against my better judgment I might add."

Jessica pushed her chair away from the table and jumped to her feet. "Don't bother." She turned away before I could say anything else and ran toward the parking lot.

If I didn't know better I'd say she was jealous. Then again, maybe I just pissed her off as much as she pissed me off.

***

I was waiting in front of the parking lot and did a double take when Cathy drove up in her Miata. It was covered in black spots and obviously designed to look like a Holstein cow. The Wisconsin license plate read, "MOOOOO."

I opened the door and climbed in. "When you said you would drive I had no idea what I was letting myself in for."

"It's my statement of absolute cow nonsense," Cathy said.

"But why?" I asked.

She popped the clutch and my sore shoulder slammed against the door as she raced across the parking lot. A bolt of pain ran up and down my arm and I felt light-headed.

With the pain came the realization that I probably should have stayed home and spent the night recuperating, but I was intrigued by Cathy. Her eccentricity, or maybe it was just plain weirdness, reminded me of the people I'd most enjoyed interacting with in Key West.

"I used to collect cow things. You know, ice cream scoops that mooed, trinkets of all kinds. I never had to buy any; once friends found out I collected cow stuff it was like open season. The things just kept flowing in. When I decided to get out of Wisconsin I opted for a new car. This was it. My ex hasn't seen it yet, but I'm sure he'll hate it."

"I'm surprised you were able to find someone to paint the damn thing," I said.

She grinned. "Actually, I tried three different auto paint shops and when they found out what I wanted to do they acted like I was crazy and turned me away. Finally someone suggested I get some of the 3M sticky vinyl stuff and do it myself, so I did. I used black trash bags to cut my patterns."

We left the marina, drove down a gravel road, past a junk yard, and turned onto a four lane highway labeled Dauphin Island Parkway, referred to as D.I.P. by the locals. I soon discovered the true meaning of driving a car that looks like a cow. The top was down and when we stopped at the first light I heard a distinct "Moo" from the car to my right. I looked over and got a thumbs-up from the teenager driving the car. In the back seat another youth stuck his head out of the window and again let loose with a loud "Moo."

At the next light, it was an older couple who couldn't resist the spectacle of a cow car. The man driving shook his head and said something to his passenger. Her door shot open and she ran to the front of their car. Pointing a camera at us she snapped our picture, and skipped back to her door with a wave.

"This happen often?" I asked.

"Constantly," Cathy said. "It's what makes the car so much fun. Does it bother you?"

"It's a bit disconcerting," I admitted.

We turned onto Interstate 10, and by the time we reached Highway 65, three cars and a truck had honked at us. I found myself slouching a little in my seat, which aggravated the cuts on my shoulder.

The Blues Cafe was a rundown concrete box that didn't quite fit in among the retail stores and car dealerships. It was six-thirty and the parking lot was just beginning to fill. Cathy pulled in between a new Harley and a Dodge Ram pickup, turned off the car, and faced me.

"Just so you know, Wes, this is who I am. I like the attention this car brings me. I like you, I think we can have some fun together, but what you see is what you get."

"I can handle it."

"You sure? I saw you scooting down when those cars were honking at us."

My insecurities were battling my hormones at the moment. I took a deep breath and let it out slowly. "So maybe it will take a little while to get used to riding around in a cow car."

Cathy nodded and swung open her door. She looked up at the sky and climbed out of the car. "I think I'll leave the top down. It doesn't look like it's going to rain tonight."

Inside, the cafe was dark and smoky, the tables clustered close together. A small dance floor and band stage cluttered the front of the room. Behind the dance floor another room opened up where two pool tables sat, and a third room led off to the right. We chose a table next to the bar, ordered a couple of beers, and asked when the mudbugs would be served.

"It's self-serve, honey." The waitress who set our beers in front of us looked like she wasn't old enough to be out alone at night. She wore low-rider jeans, a cutoff t-shirt, and sported a jeweled belly ring. "When you see 'em starting to line up over to the right there, y'all know they're fixing to eat. Follow the crowd and you can't go wrong."

Like an angry genie trapped in a bottle, Clarence "Frogman" Henry wailed out from the jukebox. Cathy leaned close to me, touched my hand, and whispered, "I don't think I've ever seen this many middle-aged men with ponytails walking around in one place. And every woman seems to come equipped with a pack of cigarettes and a long neck bottle of beer."

I nodded. "Bikers and rednecks. This was your pick, remember. I assumed you'd been here before."

"Nope. I heard some of the regulars at the bar talking about this place and I thought it would be interesting. It's obvious I'm not in Mazo anymore."

"Mazo?"

She laughed, moved her hand from my arm, and picked up her beer. "Mazomanie, Wisconsin. Population one thousand four hundred and eighty-four."

"You still have family there?" I asked.

"Nope." Cathy's smile turned to a frown and she slammed her empty beer bottle down and stood. "Looks like the line's forming." She reached out for my hand, urged me up, and led me across the room.

We drifted up to the serving table, heaped spicy crawfish, steamed corn, and potatoes onto paper plates, and made our way through the gathering crowd back to our table. Cathy didn't say much, and it was obvious to me that I had hit a sore spot when I asked about her family. While I debated whether I should apologize, she set her plate down, put her hands on her hips, and stuck her tongue out at me. I couldn't help smiling.

"Look, I have issues with my past. I know it, and now you know it. What say we talk about something else? Maybe after I get to know you a little better, we can get back to that subject."

"Fair enough." I sat down, caught the waitress's attention, and ordered a couple more beers. "Now, how about if you show me how to eat these buggers. I'm starving."

She gave me a sleepy smile and reached for a mudbug. "First you grab the head, snap it down and off, then you pinch the tail here." She grabbed the tail where it bent, squeezed it, caught the meat in her teeth where the head had been pulled off, and mumbled, "Now you pull out the meat and voilá. The locals suck the juice out of the head. I tried it once and decided to stick with the tails."

Once I felt comfortable with the process I glanced over at her. "They're good, but it seems like a lot of work for a little meat."

"I know what you mean, but they can be addictive. I chow down on them at least once a week," she said.

We finished our mudbugs and hauled the shells to the trash as the band started playing. The man on keyboard, a gray-haired, heavyset fellow who appeared to have been around, was great. The lead singer was a bit young and a little off key, but he could play the harmonica. The bass player was more than adequate and fit my image of a blues-man the best. He wore a floppy, full-brimmed hat, and an oversized jacket. He tended to tug on his beard when he wasn't playing, and possessed a mournful aura that had etched itself upon his face.

An aging black couple wearing matching leather jackets moved out onto the floor and began dancing. They held each other close and swayed together with a well-practiced rhythm. A big-breasted young woman with short cropped hair and dressed in jeans that pulled across her rear end dragged a tall, gangly man with skinny tattooed arms and a pinched, ugly face away from his beer and joined them.

"Do you dance?" Cathy asked.

I leaned forward, so she could hear me over the band. "I do a pretty good Two Step, and I can do an East Coast or West Coast Swing."

"That's great," she said. "Nobody down here seems to do West Coast Swing. Want to give it a whirl?"

We headed up to the dance floor where we spent much of the next three hours. Despite the pain in my shoulder, I was enjoying myself and felt at ease with Cathy. As we headed back to the marina, Cathy asked me what brought me to Mobile.

"Two weeks ago I learned that my father, who I never met by the way, was born and raised around here. My mother never told me much about my father and I was curious, so I sailed up here. Seems I have a whole set of relatives I didn't even know existed."

"Is that good or bad?"

I shrugged. "I haven't decided yet. Ask me in a week or so."

Cathy wasn't finished with her questions though. As we pulled into the lot Cathy parked the car and shifted her body to face me. "So you're here to meet your family?"

"Let's just say curiosity drew me here. You know what they say about curiosity. The truth is, if I hadn't met you I'm not sure I'd still be hanging around."

Cathy swung her door open and stepped out of the car. "Walk me down to the river, will you?"

"Sure," I said. As I came around the car she took my hand and we headed for the river.

Cathy gave my hand a gentle squeeze. "I had a good time tonight, Wes."

"Me too," I said. And I had. I also had high expectations of where the conversation might lead us until I saw who was sitting at the gathering table under the restaurant.

Without thinking I took her arm and started to steer Cathy around the other side of the building when a voice called out, "Hey Cuz, come on over and join us." As she lifted a beer bottle in greeting the person across from her turned so that I could see him. It was Rusty Dawson.

Chapter 5

Cathy pulled away from me and stopped. "I should get back to my boat."

"It's just my cousin and Rusty," I said. "We'll say a quick hi and then we can go sit by the river."

"Some other time." Cathy spun away and hurried toward the far dock where she kept her houseboat.

I walked over to the table and Rusty stood. "I was just keeping the lady company until you returned." He picked up several empty cans and started toward the parking lot.

"See you Rusty," I called out to his back as I sat down opposite my cousin. "It's almost midnight and you just ruined what promised to be a pleasant night."

Jessica raised her beer. "Sorry I can't offer you one but Rusty emptied the pack. The man sure can drink."

I glared at her until she lowered her eyes, and then I reached out and took the bottle from her hand. I downed what was left in two gulps and set the bottle aside. "What are you doing here, Jess?"

Her head snapped up. "The name's Jessica. Not Jess. Not Jessie. Jessica."

"Let me rephrase my question. What are you doing here Jessica?"

"You know how to pick a lock, Cuz?"

Dog River Blues

I knew I shouldn't ask, but I couldn't help myself. "What are you planning, Jess?" Her nose flared and before she could say anything I added, "I mean Jessica."

"I spent the afternoon trying to track down Sam Quinlin. I drove by his office and there were three newspapers sitting in front of the door. I don't think he's been around for a few days. I thought if we could get inside we could look for the book."

"That's crazy," I said.

"Why?"

"You don't even know that Quinlin was involved."

Jessica chewed on her lower lip and gave me a look that seemed to question my sanity. "Why won't he return my calls?"

"Because you're a pest."

Jessica jumped up, knocking over her chair in the process. "I was hoping because you were family you would help."

"I don't think you've really thought this out, Jessica. Why don't you go to the police and let them handle it."

"I'm gonna get the book back with or without your help. Just like Granddaddy asked."

"You're liable to end up in jail."

Jessica moved around the table to stand in front of me. "I wouldn't want you to take any chances, Cuz. I'll figure out how to get into the building myself."

As she started off toward the parking lot I thought I heard her sniffle. Was she crying? Would she really break into the building by herself? I decided she would.

"Wait," I called out.

Jessica stopped and as she turned she reached up and wiped her nose with the back of her hand.

I stood. "If I agree to this there are some ground rules."

"Such as."

"I'll go in and check the place out while you stand watch."

"I don't think so."

"I need to know if anyone shows up."

"You don't know what the book looks like."

"How many five-hundred-year-old books is Quinlin likely to be keeping in his office?"

"All right, we'll do it your way."

"I really don't expect to find the book lying around Quinlin's office."

"Then why are you agreeing to come along?"

"I don't know. Maybe I have Batman syndrome or something. But just because I'm not willing to let you do this on your own doesn't mean I think this is a good idea." I paused for effect and added, "You'll have to drive. I don't have a car."

It began to rain as we drove away from the marina. With the rain came cooler temperatures. Thunder rattled the night. Spasms of pain ran through my shoulder and I began to shiver. I wondered if it was the cold, or the anticipation of what I was about to do.

I'd made my decision to go along with Jessica's plan reluctantly. I knew the chances of finding anything useful were small in comparison with the possibility of being caught breaking into Quinlin's office, but I couldn't let

Jessica do this alone. She wasn't equipped for this type of action. All I could do was hope that this trip would give me at least a clue as to what was going on.

It was a little after midnight when we drove by Sam Quinlin's office. "That's it." Jessica pointed to a small house that must have been converted into an office somewhere along the line.

"Turn there." I pointed to a side street a half block past the parking lot.

Jessica turned, drove another half block and swung into a parking space across from a small park. We climbed out of the car and walked back to the office.

"It looks like there's a light on in the back," Jessica said. "Do you think Sam's working late?"

"Let's go around to the front," I said. "We may get to talk to the elusive gentleman after all."

We moved from the back of the building to the front. There were two curtained windows along the side of the building. One was lit. The other was dark. My heart raced like an out of control engine, and my hands were clammy by the time we reached the front of the building. Adding to my anxiety, the lot was well lit and two cars drove by as we crept up to the door.

The door was ajar, the latch holding it from closing. I reached for the doorknob. "It looks like someone didn't pull the door tight when they left."

"Are you going in?" Jessica asked.

"Remember our deal," I said. "You can watch the lot from around the corner of the building. If the police or anyone else shows up, knock on the window and head for the car. I'll find the back door and be right behind you."

Jessica reached out and touched my arm. "Be careful, Wes."

I patted her hand, pushed open the door, and stopped to listen. Nothing, but the gut-wrenching smell emanating from somewhere within caused me to hesitate.

"What's wrong," Jessica asked.

"Go around to the back of the building and wait for me there."

"Why."

"Goddamn it Jessica. Will you just do what I ask for once?"

She muttered something about assholes and cavemen as she moved away from me. I waited until she disappeared around the corner before opening the door and stepping into the office.

Easing the door closed behind me I made sure that the latch rested as it had when we'd arrived. If I had to make a quick exit I didn't want to worry about the lock.

The thick, coppery smell of dried blood permeated the building. Despite the coolness of the night, I found myself wiping sweat from my brow. I could hear the clock over the sofa as it ticked away the seconds and the fluorescent lighting gave the walls a tarnished look.

I crept toward the back office and froze when I heard the distant sound of a siren. I had spent a lot of years chasing criminals but I was uncomfortable with my new role. I was not cut out to be a burglar.

Dragging out my handkerchief, I used it to cover my nose and mouth before opening the office door. My stomach churned and I knew what I was going to find.

I've never gotten used to the sight or the smell of violent death. I assumed it was Sam Quinlin's body sprawled out on the carpet in front of me. This explained why he hadn't returned any of Jessica's calls. There was no doubt the man on the floor was dead, there was no need to check for a pulse. I wanted to go through the desk, but the room was small and I couldn't get around the body without risking stepping in the dead man's blood.

As I backed into the main office, a deep voice boomed out from behind me. "Don't touch anything."

I spun around, tripped, and fought to keep my balance. Before I could tumble backward toward the body, a giant hand shot out and caught my arm.

The man facing me was perhaps six-two with broad shoulders, narrow hips, and arms that seemed almost too long for his body. His brown hair was splashed with gray and tied back in a ponytail. His face was tanned and lined from too many hours spent in the sun. He wore khaki pants and a camouflage hunting jacket.

He pushed me out of the way and bent over the body. "This Quinlin?"

"That's my guess. You a cop?"

He glared at me. "I look like a cop?"

"No."

"Good, 'cause if I were a cop I'd be arresting you right about now. Let's get the hell out of here before one turns up."

"If you're not a cop, who are you?"

"I'm your Uncle Roy, son. But we really ain't got time for introductions right now. The police could be on their way for all we know. Did you touch anything besides the two door knobs?"

"No."

"Good." He held out his hand. "Give me your hankie." I handed it to him and then watched as he wiped the office doorknob and then hustled across the floor to the outer door. He waited until I'd stepped outside, then he wiped that knob before swinging the door closed shut behind him.

"I sent Jessica home," Roy said. I followed as he began to jog around the building. Ahead I could make out the silhouette of my cousin as she climbed into her car. Parked behind her was a monstrosity of a truck. "You come with me," he added. "We gotta talk."

Once we were on our way I asked, "How the hell did you know we were here?"

"Jessica asked me to come along and I told her no. Told her it was a bad idea and made her promise not to do it. I got to thinking about how well Jessica listens so I went looking for her. I didn't expect her to find some idiot who would go along with her hair-brained idea."

"Have you ever tried to tell that girl no?"

He looked at me and grinned. "Many times. Like I said, that's why I came down here myself. She can get herself in trouble without even trying."

I reached into my pocket, took out my cell phone and opened it.

"Who are you calling?" Uncle Roy asked.

"I was going to call the police. They need to know Sam Quinlin's dead."

He reached out and snatched the phone from my hands. "We don't want them tracing your phone. We can stop at a pay phone if you gotta call, but if I had my druthers, I'd let someone else find the body."

"Why?"

"I don't like the government getting involved in my life or my family's lives. They're insidious. We don't have any freedoms any more. The government spies on us constantly. It's why I don't use the damn cell phone Jessica gave me."

"And to think, Jessica told me you were crazy."

"That may be open for discussion. I don't much like people. I find if I act a little nuts then I get left alone. Jessica's one of the few people I can stand being around for any length of time. That's why I wasn't going to let her get hurt. Or worse."

"I kept her outside and I would have kept her away if I could have."

"I know," he said. "She's hard-headed, that's for sure. Drives Ben right up the wall. Where do I need to take you?"

I gave him directions to the Bay View Marina and sat back in the seat. I wasn't sure whether I was glad that Roy had shown up or not. Sam Quinlin's murder had ratcheted up my interest. I wished I'd gone through the office, but if the book had ever been there it was likely that whoever killed Quinlin had it now.

This had gone way beyond what Jessica could handle, and it didn't look like she was going to let it go. I still wasn't sure how I felt about the family thing; it would take awhile to get used to. But I was involved now, whether I liked it or not.

I might not know who had the book or why Sam Quinlin was dead, but I knew one person who might have some answers—Fish Conners. It was about time he and I had a talk.

Chapter 6

A dark wave of loneliness washed over me as the taillights on Roy's truck disappeared from view. A northern breeze had picked up and it sent a chill through me like a ghostly omen. I was troubled and perhaps a little confused. I already had a dysfunctional relationship with my mother. Did I really need more relatives cluttering up my life?

I'd grown up without ever knowing this family existed. I was pissed at my mother for not telling me about them, and at Jessica for drawing me into a situation I wasn't sure I wanted. How do you develop familial feelings for people who were never a part of your life?

I don't know what I expected when I brought the boat to Mobile, but it wasn't what I found. There was the gorgeous cousin who spoke like a hillbilly one minute and a well-educated femme fatale the next. Add in an uncle who waited until he was fifty to find his calling as a Catholic priest, and another who looked like an aging hippy. Oh, and let's not forget the grandfather who was a thief and the father who seemed to have disappeared from the face of the earth. I wasn't sure I could survive meeting my grandmother. I had visions of her sitting in a rocking chair smoking a corncob pipe with a shotgun resting across her knees.

As I headed down the dock I was so wrapped up in my thoughts that I didn't notice the figure sitting on the bench in front of the closed marina store until a voice called out, "Hey."

I jumped at the unexpected sound, drew a deep breath, and moved into a protective crouch. To my relief I realized the voice belonged to Cathy.

"Didn't mean to scare you." Cathy stood and the movement triggered a motion sensor that switched on a pair of lights situated on either side of the doorway.

"What are you doing out here?" I asked.

She still had on the jeans she'd worn when we were out dancing but she'd added a snug-fitting white sweatshirt with a picture of Rudolf the Red Nosed Reindeer on the front.

"Waiting for you. I felt bad taking off on you like I did this evening. I walked down to your boat and knocked. When you didn't answer I came up here to wait. I was just about to head home."

I noticed an abstract dusting of something dark on the shoulder of the shirt, and without thinking, I brushed it away, and she stepped in close to me. "You're walking like you're in pain. I noticed it earlier too, when we were dancing."

"I had an unexpected visitor last night." I gave her a quick rundown of what had happened after I left the restaurant.

"Who was it?"

"I think he was a local guy by the name of Fish Conners, but I can't swear to it."

Cathy reached out and placed her hand against my chest. When I winced she drew a breath and whispered in a hoarse, excited voice, "Let me see what he did to you."

The cold air nipped at me as I started to pull up my shirt. She pushed my hands away and lifted the edge herself. "Jesus," she said.

Her hands were icy, the air cold, and a shiver ran down my body as she unbuttoned my shirt. She touched the largest bruise that started at my belly button and traced it with her finger up across my left nipple to where it ended just below my neckline. "Does it hurt?"

"Not right now," I said. My heart raced as she opened her hand and placed her palm against the skin of my chest. She moved her lips up to mine and leaned in to kiss me. Her lips had a faint, salty taste.

My body tingled and I returned the kiss. An electric charge ran down to my knees, making them feel weak and useless. Her hair brushed my nose. It tickled and carried the scent of apple blossom shampoo and lingering cigarette smoke from the bar. When she pulled away I swayed as if I'd just chugged a bottle of strawberry wine.

"Come on. I'll walk you down to your boat," she said.

Afraid that anything I might say would break the mood, I just nodded. When she took my hand I let her lead me down the dock and into the cockpit of my boat.

As I removed the washboards that covered the doorway she took off my shirt and began to unbuckle my belt. After that it took a conscious effort on my part to snap the plastic door cover in place, and as we entered the cabin she began tugging at my shorts like a playful kitten.

We fumbled with each other's clothes between kisses, and then stood in the center of the cabin among our scattered clothing, entwined in a hungry embrace. When I couldn't stand it any longer I put my hands on her shoulders and guided her to the front berth where I watched her appreciatively as she climbed naked into my bed.

I did my best to ignore the pain that racked my body as we made love twice that night. The first time was quick and peppered with wild shouts and energetic maneuverings. The second time was long and slow and tender, and afterward we fell asleep in each other's arms.

I awoke to a soft knocking on the hull of my boat. "Hold on just a minute," I called out as I slid off the berth and searched the floor for my shorts. I started to shiver as soon as I moved into the cockpit. I wished I'd grabbed my sweatshirt.

"Hey, Rusty." I pushed the plastic door covering closed behind me and longed for the warmth of my bed and Cathy's naked body beneath the covers. Still, I wanted to be neighborly. "I can put on a pot of coffee if you want?"

"No thanks." He looked down from the dock at my bruised body, and then shifted his attention to meet my eyes. "I've got to get going, but I picked up some information on Fish Conners I thought you might like to have."

I started to reply but hesitated when I saw Rusty's eyes widen. At the same time, I felt the plastic door cover shift behind me, and Cathy stepped out into the cockpit, crowding me forward.

"How you doing today, Rusty?" she asked. He nodded a greeting and frowned at her.

"Here," she added, handing me the shirt I had worn the previous evening. "You'll freeze to death dressed like that."

I turned to look at her and saw that she was dressed in one of my t-shirts. Her nipples were hard from the cold, and I lost all interest in Fish Conners, or Rusty, for that matter. "You should talk," I said, as she ducked back into the cabin.

"I didn't know you two were an item," Rusty said, as I threw on the shirt.

I made a slight motion with my shoulder, a non-committal shrug. "Things happen," I said. "But I'm not sure you could call us an item at this point."

Rusty shook his head. "Whatever. All I know is that this is going to be prime scuttlebutt for the rumor mongers up at the round table."

"Cathy must not be too worried about it," I said. "She didn't have to come out here and let you see her like that." I was beginning to feel uncomfortable standing there under his scrutiny, so I shifted his attention back to Fish Conners. "Did you say you had some information for me?"

"Yes sir, I do." Rusty cleared his throat, turned his head, and spit into the river. "I heard Fish hangs out at a little dive of a bar not far from here. Place called Darlene's. Friday night's raw oyster night. Way I hear it Fish loves them, especially when they're free. 'Course I also hear tell he drinks enough to more than pay for them."

"Want to take a ride down there with me tonight?" I asked.

"Sorry, no can do. I gotta go to Biloxi today. Be gone 'till tomorrow, but you'll have no trouble finding the place. I wrote down the directions." He reached over, handed me a slip of paper, and spit out of the corner of his mouth again before turning and sauntering down the dock.

"What was that all about?" Cathy was standing in the doorway and to my disappointment she was dressed and looked like she was ready to leave.

"Oysters," I said. She frowned at my flippancy, and I added, "Rusty knows about this trouble with my cousin and all and he knew I was looking for Fish Conners. He told me where I might be able to find him."

Cathy slid around me as I moved out of the way. "I've got to get going," she said.

"I was hoping we might get a chance to talk a little before you left," I said.

"About what?"

I pointed a finger at Cathy, and then at me. "Us. What happened."

Cathy shook her head and ran her fingers like a comb through her mussed hair. She sighed, plopped down on the cockpit seat, and patted the space next to her. I sat down.

She took my hand and held it on her lap. "Look, Wes, I like you. Obviously I find you attractive or we wouldn't have ended up in bed together. And the sex was very, very good. But to be honest, I'm still in love with my ex-husband."

"You could have told me that before we went out." I knew when I spoke it wasn't the right thing to say, but I was irritated and couldn't help myself.

"You know, when I agreed to go out with you it wasn't exactly a lifetime commitment. I like bad boys, and the ex is a bad boy," she said. "Actually, he's an actor. They don't always work steady. He sold some pot to a couple of other actors and got busted. He's getting out of jail tomorrow."

"Sorry," I said. I'd been chastised. "And last night?"

She stroked my hand, brought it up to her lips and kissed it before looking me in the eyes. "Last night you were my bad boy." She reached out and touched my bruise through my shirt. "You told me about your fight, showed me your pain, and I melted. I'm not saying it can't happen again. But I'm being honest when I tell you it will be for fun, not forever. If you can accept that, then we can get together again. If not, then we end things right here."

I nodded, but I knew it wouldn't work for me. I just couldn't say that to her.

"Good," she said. "Now I've got to get going." She leaned forward and kissed me on the cheek, letting her lips linger for just a moment. We broke apart and both stood at the same time, as if our actions were choreographed.

I didn't watch her leave, just swayed with the quick movement of the boat as she stepped onto the dock. I felt strangely calm for a man who'd just had his ego deflated by a very sexy woman.

Chapter 7

I've suffered on and off from depression ever since a young girl died because of a mistake I made. Celine Stewart still came to me in my dreams. She never spoke, she just pleaded with me through sad eyes, silently accusing me of screwing up.

When I'd first been diagnosed, my doctor recommended Prozac, but the idea of using any kind of mind-altering drug had little appeal to me. I rejected his offer of medicated bliss and instead turned to my lifelong love of sailing for relief. Still, on occasion, I suffer episodes of darkness where the light dims and threatens to go out. This is often followed by roller coaster flights of fancy and bravado. Today, all I wanted to do was sleep.

A distant beat tore me from dark dreams where that ghost taunted me. Looking around the room I felt dazed until I realized that the music was the call of my cell phone.

I reached over, picked it up, and when I saw the number, put it back down. The last person I wanted to talk to was Jessica. I rolled over and went back to sleep.

Once again it was my phone that woke me. Once again it was Jessica.

I flipped it open. "What do you want?"

"Where have you been? I've been trying to get hold of you all day."

"I was sleeping."

"It's after five."

"Did you call for a reason, or just to check on my sleeping habits?"

I felt a twinge of guilt as I listened to her breathing on the other end. When she spoke again there was a sharp edge to her voice. "I wanted to see how you were doing and to find out what our next step is."

"Nothing."

"What do you mean?"

"I'm done. Let the old man handle things. He seems competent."

"Uncle Roy? I never expected him to show up last night. He doesn't really want to get involved."

"Neither do I."

"You can't back out now," she said.

"Watch me." I switched off the phone and flung it across the cabin where it bounced off the settee and landed on the floor with a dull thud. I knew I was being irrational, but with dead bodies came responsibility. I didn't want to be responsible for another girl's death, especially a relative I barely knew.

I thought about going back to bed. I thought about the warm inviting beaches of the Bahamas. I thought about untying the boat and taking off. Instead, I headed down to the marina store for a cold six-pack.

I paid for the Miller Lite and left the building by the side door leading to the gathering area. I couldn't stand the thought of drinking alone on my boat but wasn't sure I was up to idle chitchat either.

I'd met most of the locals the first afternoon I spent at the marina. Bob Preston, known around the marina as Cajun Bob, saw me and waved me over. Cajun Bob lived on a steel trawler he built himself and worked some kind of construction job. He was short and in his mid-thirties. He kept his long black hair tied back in a ponytail, had a thick, weightlifters body, and an even thicker Cajun accent, which earned him his nickname.

Bob seemed to be the name of the day in these parts. In the short time I'd been at the marina I'd also met Motorcycle Bob, Too Tall Bob, Lil Bob, and a generic Bob who had apparently not earned a nickname yet.

I sat down across from Cajun Bob. Phil Hamlin and his wife, Renee, were seated to his right. Phil was a potbellied, balding, retired stockbroker. Renee, thin, with bottle-tinted red hair and disapproving eyes was the marina gossip. She tended to dress in garish skin-tight pants that accentuated her bony frame, and spoke with a husky, sexual voice that fit neither her body nor her personality.

They'd come down from Illinois on a thirty-seven foot Beneteau sloop with the intention of sailing around the world. That was three years ago and marina rumor had it that they'd never had the sails up on the boat and never even run the engine since arriving at the Dog River.

"What's this I hear about you and Cathy?" Cajun Bob asked. He wore a knowing smirk on his face, and I wanted to reach out and snatch it away.

"Don't put much store in what people say around here," Phil said.

"Waitresses tend to be slutty." Renee was knitting something that could have been a sweater, and didn't bother to look up when she spoke.

"You were a waitress in college," Phil said.

"For only two weeks." She looked up for a moment and cast an evil look at Phil. "You know I quit because I didn't like hanging around with those girls."

"I thought the boss fired you because you were too slow," Phil said.

Again Renee looked up from her work. Her eyes found Phil's, and she held his gaze for a full count of ten before turning her attention back to her work. This time the look must have worked. Phil picked up his beer bottle and took a deep slug before setting it back down. The silence between the two was more telling than their verbal sparring.

"I took a swing at the lady myself," Cajun Bob said. "We just haven't been able to get together yet." He watched me for a reaction and when I didn't jump at the bait he continued. "Course if you two have something going I'll step back out of the running."

"That's nice of you, Bob." I was saved further discourse by the arrival of my cousin Jessica. Her car skidded to a stop at the edge of the parking lot. I sipped my beer and watched her throw open the door and spring from the car.

She wore white jeans with a tight white blouse and her breasts bounced madly as she strode up to where I was seated. "You're a son of a bitch, Wes Darling."

"You move pretty damn fast for someone who's only been here a few days," Cajun Bob said.

I thought I detected a tone of approval in his voice. It was a sense of regard I could do without. He was a shallow man with a shallow agenda. "She's my cousin," I said.

"This is Alabama," Cajun Bob said.

I turned and glared at him. "Shut up, Bob, before I get really pissed and do something I'll regret."

"I was just...."

"Didn't you hear the man?" Jessica asked, without looking away from me. "If Wes doesn't take a swing at you, I just might." Her anger was directed at me as much as at Cajun Bob.

"You want to take a ride?" I asked.

"Sure." She threw me her keys and added, "Why don't you drive?"

I pushed the remaining beers into the center of the table, said, "Help yourselves," and followed Jessica out to her car.

Neither of us spoke until we were out of the parking lot. "Where are we going?" she asked.

"We're going looking for Fish Conners."

I glanced her way and read the confusion on her face. "What made you change your mind?" she asked.

"I find Cajun Bob to be a bore. Besides, Fish Conners has pissed me off more than you have in the last couple of days." I turned the car onto Dauphin Island Parkway and reached into my pocket for the directions Rusty had given me. I drew them out and handed them to Jessica. "You navigate," I said.

It was starting to get dark so Jessica turned on the dome light. After a minute she tucked the paper into the visor and switched off the light. "I've been to Darlene's," she said. "Make a left at the next light, then a left at the stop sign and follow the road around. You can't miss it. What makes you think Fish will be there?"

"Rusty Dawson told me Fish goes out there on free oyster night. That's tonight."

"What do we do if he's there?"

I pulled into Darlene's lot, parked the car, and got out without answering her question. Truth of the matter was, I wasn't sure what I was going to do. I just wanted to see the guy up close. Maybe ask him why he tried to kill me.

The bar's décor was a mix of vintage pub and modern sports bar. The jukebox looked like it was from a fifties malt shop, but it had been converted to play CDs. The wood floor was scarred and polished by years of foot traffic. The bar appeared to have gone through a recent facelift. Three television sets hung from the ceiling above the bar, and new wood tables with vinyl-covered chairs were scattered about. I suspected it wouldn't be long before the owner managed to kill the Southern ambiance and replace it with anywhere USA dull.

The place was packed and I took one of only two empty seats at the bar, next to a tall redhead dressed in jeans and a t-shirt with the words "Hell Bound" stenciled across her abundant chest. She looked over at me, picked up her beer, and tipped the long neck in my direction. I nodded, and then watched her glow evaporate as Jessica took the seat next to me.

Jessica put her lips close to my ear and exhaled, sending a pleasant chill down my back. "They're probably fake."

I spun the bar stool to face her. "I didn't notice."

"Right. And you just happened to sit in the seat right next to Miss Jumbo Tits?"

"There were only two empty seats at the bar."

"I noticed you left me the seat next to Sasquatch."

I looked over at the bearded giant seated next to her and laughed. "So, all right, maybe I did choose this seat because of the scenery, but we're not here for fun. Do you see Fish Conners around?"

Jessica was peering over my shoulder while I studied the room behind her. After a few moments she poked me in the arm. "Over there, by the jukebox."

I followed her gaze and watched as the man who'd tried to kill me sat down at a table. He was dressed in khaki Dockers, wore gold chains around his neck, and had left the top three buttons of his shirt undone. If he was the man who had attacked me on the dock, he was also much bigger than I remembered him.

I swung my barstool around and slid off at the same time he noticed us. He grinned and pushed back his chair, jumped up, and hustled toward the back of the bar. We followed, weaving our way between clumps of bar patrons. He beat us to the rear door by a half dozen steps and pushed through it, letting it swing closed behind him.

"You wait here," I said when we reached the door. "I don't want to have to worry about you getting hurt."

"Are you nuts? The guy's built like a truck. If you go out there he'll bulldoze his way right through you."

I reached for the door. "What did you think was going to happen if we found him?"

"I don't know," she said. "But I don't want you to get hurt either."

"Just wait here and call out an alarm if it looks like I need help. Or call the police. Who knows? Maybe the guy will just talk to me about the whole thing and we'll find out he went after the wrong person."

Jessica muttered something about men and their crazy macho attitudes. I took a deep breath, swung the door open, and stepped outside.

"Wes!" Jessica called out from the doorway.

He must have been hiding alongside the door. I spun around but I wasn't fast enough. Fish Conners drove his shoulder into my mid-section with the force of a demolition ball. He half carried, half pushed me across the dirt yard, smashing my body into the concrete block wall of the building. I'd played football in high school, but the force of Fish's body block was like nothing I'd ever felt before.

Fish backed away, and I slid down the wall. My legs were too weak to support me and when I tried to push myself up my entire body rebelled. I fought to remain alert.

Conners looked down at me and never said a word. He just smiled. He drew back his foot and lashed out at my head. I moved aside just enough so that he missed my face and hit his foot against the wall. He cursed and prepared to take another shot at me, when out of the darkness appeared the white, angel-like form of my cousin.

In a flash she was on Fish's back. Kicking and screaming, she dug her manicured nails into his face and eyes, drawing his attention away from me.

Fish whirled about and tried to shake her loose, but Jessica clung to his back like a cowgirl out to break her first mustang. Fish bucked again, then grabbed her leg, and tore Jessica from his back. He studied her for a moment, decided she wasn't worth bothering with, and then threw her across the dirt lot.

Jessica's attack had lasted less than a minute, but it was enough time for me to catch my breath. As Fish turned his attention back to me I looked around and spotted a small pile of wood over by the trashcan.

I lunged toward it, conscious of the harsh sound of his footsteps. Unsure of how close Fish was, I dove at the pile and came up with a short piece of two-by-four. Crouching low I turned, expecting to find my opponent right behind me. Fish was nowhere to be seen. A small crowd from the bar had gathered outside to see what the commotion was and must have scared him off. I let out a sigh of relief and despite my aching back and knees, I hobbled over to the prone body of my cousin. Jessica let out a groan and rolled over as I knelt down. Before I could decide what to do, the tall redhead joined me at Jessica's side.

"I'm a nurse," she said. She ran a hand over Jessica's arms and legs like a psychic healer and added, "There don't appear to be any broken bones." The woman used her thumb and forefinger to lift Jessica's right eyelid and my cousin moaned and pulled away.

"What's going on?" the redhead asked.

"Just a personal spat." Jessica pushed herself into a seated position and glared at the woman through gritted teeth. "Not really any of your business."

The redhead got to her feet. "Good. I guess I can get back to my beer then." I watched as she pushed her way through the horde of gawkers that were milling about. As if on cue, the crowd broke up and followed her through the doorway.

"She was only trying to help," I pointed out.

Jessica climbed to her feet and looked down at her stained white jeans. "Next thing you know she'd a been wanting to call the cops. Down here we handle things in our own way. You know, when I asked you for help the other day I didn't expect to be the one coming to the rescue. I was afraid Fish was going to run you right through that wall."

"You wouldn't have had to come to my rescue if you'd done what I asked. Didn't I tell you to get some help if it looked like I was in trouble?"

She shrugged her shoulders and then gasped at the pain it caused her. "I guess I didn't think. I saw him pounding on you and I just reacted. Besides, I was afraid that if I left you'd be dead by the time I got back. So now what do we do?"

"I suggest we go back to the marina and talk about that over a beer." As I started to walk around the building toward the car Jessica began to laugh.

"What's so funny?" I asked.

She limped up alongside me, put her arm through mine and said, "No one will ever accuse us of being Sherlock Holmes and Watson, will they?"

"I guess not," I said. "Let's go get that drink."

Chapter 8

Although the marina restaurant was about half-full, there were no customers at the bar. As Jessica and I took a seat there, Cathy tossed her towel into the sink and headed our way. For a woman who wasn't really interested in me, she managed to convey her irritation as she set a coaster in front of Jessica. "You're the cousin, I guess?"

Jessica slipped her arm through mine. "Kissin' cousins, really. Ain't that right, Cuz?"

"Well, not really." I was embarrassed by the implication, and I tried to disengage from Jessica's grip. She clutched my arm like I was a wayward child, and I gave in and stopped struggling.

"I guess Wes has become localized a lot faster than I did," Cathy said.

"No I haven't." I jerked my arm and this time Jessica released it. "She's kidding. There's nothing like that going on between us."

"Kind of quick to deny it," Cathy said. "Makes me wonder."

"He's easily embarrassed," Jessica said.

Cathy put out her hand. "Name's Cathy."

When Jessica reached out to take the offered hand I stood and excused myself to go to the bathroom. I didn't know how I felt about these two women suddenly getting friendly. I was pretty sure it could only lead to more aggravation for me. I wished I smoked; it would be a perfect excuse to escape the confines of the restaurant.

I took as much time as I dared before heading back. I could see the two of them bent over the bar, heads together, whispering. When Cathy saw me she waved and drifted away.

I looked down at the beer sitting in front of my stool and then glanced at Jessica. "What's up between the two of you?"

"Just a little girl talk," Jessica said. "I ordered us both Buds. Hope that's all right?"

It wasn't my favorite beer but I picked up the bottle and took a healthy slug. At least it was cold. "Not spilling any family secrets, I hope?" I asked.

Cathy joined us right then. "She gave me a quick rundown of what you've been up to. I suggested you could use a little help looking for your missing book."

I looked over at Jessica and raised an eyebrow.

"When I explained why I'm such a mess, I mentioned Fish," Jessica said. "Cathy said you told her about your first run-in."

I bit back a retort, gulped down the rest of my beer, and held up the empty bottle. "Can I get a Miller Lite this time?"

Cathy took the bottle and then reached for another. "I think you should ask your Uncle Roy for help." She popped the cap and held it out to me, but when I reached for it she pulled it away. "Maybe he can keep you from getting the shit beat out of you every other day."

I grabbed the drink from her hand and slammed it down on the counter. "This really isn't any of your business."

Cathy cast an evil eye in my direction and put her hands on her hips. "You're an asshole, Darling. I sort of feel that sleeping with you gives me a reason to worry about you."

As she turned away I called out, "You told me it didn't mean anything. That negates your rights."

I thought her shoulders slumped a little and I felt like a heel. I was about to call out an apology when Jessica leaned toward me and whispered in my ear.

"You slept with her?"

"That's none of your business."

"Fine," Jessica said, but it obviously wasn't. She picked up her beer, drained it, and slid off her stool. "I think Cathy's right."

"What? You think we should ask your Uncle Roy for his help?"

"He's your Uncle Roy too." Jessica took two steps away from the bar, then stopped and shot me an angry look. "And no, that's not what I mean. I was referring to the part about you being an asshole. Don't bother waiting for me. I've got to hit the ladies room, then I'm leaving."

Cathy moved over to where I was seated and picked up Jessica's bottle. "You should wait for her."

"I told you there's nothing going on between us."

"Maybe not on your part. Trust me Wes, you need to be waiting for her when she gets out of the head and then you need to walk her to her car."

"But..."

"She's your cousin and she's feeling dissed. Just go." Cathy picked up my half-full bottle and before I could protest she took it away.

I sat there for a minute wondering what I was getting myself into, and then I threw a twenty on the counter and moved over to the door to wait for Jessica.

She glanced past me when she came out of the ladies room, pretending I was a stranger when I opened the door for her. I followed her down the stairs and out to her car. Finally, she glanced at me, raised an eyebrow, and acknowledged my presence.

"You want me to talk to Uncle Roy?" she asked.

"I'd rather we did it together. I'd like to hear his response."

"You don't trust me?" Jessica asked, as she reached behind her and opened the car door.

"You asked me to help because I'm a trained investigator. One of the things I do is observe what goes on around me. I want to watch Roy's reaction. I don't want him involved unless he wants to be involved."

"Fine. We'll do it tomorrow night. I'll call and let you know what time I'm gonna pick you up."

"Why not in the morning?"

"Uncle Roy's a night owl. He sleeps most of the day, gets up around dinner time and doesn't go to bed until the sun comes up. I guess we could go tonight if you'd like."

I thought about it for half a second and shook my head. "I'm whipped. Every muscle in my body hurts from the beatings Fish gave me and I haven't recuperated from my boat trip up here. I did two overnight sails in a week."

"I'll call tomorrow," Jessica said.

I started to turn away but Jessica wasn't quite finished with me. She grabbed my arm and tugged until I spun to face her, then she threw her arms around my neck and locked her lips on mine.

I tried to pull away but she was a strong girl, and then I wasn't trying so hard. My mind shouted that this was so wrong, but I drew her closer and returned the kiss and just when I thought I'd found heaven, she pushed me away and jumped into her car.

Lowering the window, Jessica stuck her tongue out. "Now you know what it means to be kissin' cousins. So why don't you take your *not-me* attitude, shove it in a pipe, and smoke it."

I stood there, my body limp as a piece of overcooked spaghetti, until her taillights vanished in the night. As I headed back toward the boat I mulled over what had happened. Jessica seemed to be toying with me, and enjoying it way too much. I didn't know what the hell was going on in her mind, but my thoughts were spiraling out of control.

In the distance Lyle Lovett was playing on a stereo. The cool night air smelled of salt water, swamp mud, and shit, as if someone had just pumped their head out into the river. The moon sat in the sky and cast a near perfect glow like a magical corridor along the length of the Dog River, and I had never felt so confused in my life.

The tide was going out and it was a long step down into the cockpit of my boat. As I got ready for bed I ruminated over what had just happened. Maybe I was being too rigid in my thinking. After all, how did I know that she was really my cousin?

My mother had always claimed that all she knew about my father was his name. She was certainly capable of lying to me if she felt it would help drag me back into her fold. But this didn't feel like one of her ploys.

No, I was pretty sure that Jessica was my cousin and the thoughts I had when she'd kissed me out there in the parking lot were not good thoughts to have about a cousin. I needed to keep my distance from that girl and the best way to do that was to not be alone with her. It was definitely time to call on Uncle Roy, and the sooner the better. I didn't know if he'd really be much help in finding the book, but he sure as hell could create a buffer zone between Jessica and myself.

I plucked my cell phone from its holder and dialed Jessica's number.

"What up Cuz?" Jessica answered. There was a lilt to her voice that made me think she was laughing at me. I ignored it.

"Can we go see Roy tonight?"

"I thought you were tired?"

"I can't sleep."

"Why's that?" Her tone suggested that she knew exactly why I couldn't sleep. I didn't take the bait.

"I just want to talk to Roy. Can we do it tonight or not?"

"Sure, Cuz, but I need to stop for gas first. Give me half an hour."

Before I could respond she clicked off her phone. My hands started sweating at the thought of being alone with her again. I hoped to hell Roy would agree to help us. Someone was going to have to stand between Jessica and me, because if that girl ever kissed me like that again, there'd be no stopping me.

Chapter 9

My stomach churned at the thought of seeing Jessica and I couldn't sit still and wait. Throwing my clothes back on, I grabbed a Snickers bar from the fridge and hustled outside.

I gobbled down the candy bar as I trudged past the junkyard toward the end of the street. The chocolate bar did nothing to settle my stomach. A dog barked and my steps slowed. I looked behind me in time to see a large, mixed breed dog throw itself at the rusted yard gate.

As I walked along the road the animal followed on the other side of the fence, a growling shadow in the night. At the end of the property he let out a final bark and bounded off toward more interesting prey.

I paced back and forth along the edge of the road for ten minutes before spotting the headlights of a car in the distance. A moment later, Jessica's little Honda slid to a stop a few yards ahead of me. I ran up, pulled open the door, and climbed in.

"I didn't even see you," Jessica said as she turned the car around and headed back out to Dauphin Island Parkway. "You should dress in something lighter if you're going to go wandering down unlit streets at night."

I was dressed in jeans and a dark sweatshirt and couldn't argue with her reasoning. I wanted to avoid too much interaction with her so I drew an invisible curtain around myself and leaned against the door as far away from her as I could get in the little car. I don't know what I expected, but she didn't throw herself at me and she didn't bite, although when I looked her way I thought she had a rather smug smile on her face. I lay my head back, closed my eyes, and promptly dozed off.

The gentle braking of the car roused me from my fitful sleep. I stretched and glanced over at Jessica as she turned off the main highway. "Where are we?"

"Grand Bay," she said. "Uncle Roy has about twenty acres of mostly woodland out here." I thought she sounded a little curt.

"I'm sorry for falling asleep just now. I haven't recovered from the beatings I've taken in the last couple of days."

Jessica took her eyes off the road long enough to give me a speculative look. "You and me need to talk."

"About what happened between us earlier," I said.

"Indirectly," she said. "There's something I haven't told you about me, but we're almost at Uncle Roy's now. We'll talk later."

I shifted in my seat and looked out the window, watching the night shadows whiz by as we drove along the uneven road. We passed battered trailers and wood shanties. A burned out shack with the roof caving in stood out in the dark, and next to it sat a yellow school bus that had been converted into someone's home. The car slowed again and we turned onto a narrow dirt track. The driveway had been leveled with oyster shells that made snap, crackle, and pop sounds as we drove over them. I almost expected little elves with cereal bowls to come running out of the darkness.

Uncle Roy lived in a hand-built log cabin surrounded by dozens of pine trees. The place was small but neat, with well-crafted lines. A sturdy porch ran along the entire front of the building, and when I stepped out of the car I was overwhelmed by the aromatic scent of wood smoke and pine pitch. I thought that if heaven wasn't a sailboat floating on clear blue water, then this might be it.

Jessica walked up and stopped alongside of me. "I love it here. It's so peaceful."

"I don't know what I was expecting," I said. "But this wasn't it."

The door opened before we got to the steps and the large figure of my uncle stood silhouetted in the night. Beside him a massive bundle of fur, jowls and teeth took one look at us and bounded down the steps in a single gliding motion. I froze in my steps, but it wasn't me the beast was interested in, it was Jessica.

The dog let out a long howl and leaped up on Jessica, knocking her off balance. She laughed as the dog's paws rested on her shoulders, and she tolerated the tongue lashing her face received.

"Get down, Dwayne," Roy called out from the doorway. Dwayne looked over his shoulder as if questioning his master's sanity, but when Roy repeated the command Dwayne dropped down beside Jessica and looked up into her face.

"Dwayne used to be my dog." Jessica reached down and ruffled his fur. "He was a half-starved, skinny string bean of a pup when I found him. When we couldn't find his owners I begged Daddy to let me keep him. He agreed, but then Dwayne just kept growing and growing. When I went off to college Daddy and Uncle Roy decided he'd be better off out here."

Roy stepped back into the cabin. "Why don't you two kids come in and I'll fix us some coffee, 'less of course you'd rather have a stiff toddy, Wes?"

"Coffee's fine." I waved my hand to indicate Jessica should lead the way and as she passed me I whispered, "He doesn't seem surprised to see us."

"I called to let him know we were coming. Uncle Roy's not the kind of guy you pop in on unexpectedly. Especially in the middle of the night. He's a bit paranoid."

Great, I thought as I followed her through the door. *Just what I need.*

Inside, the cabin was as neat and trim as the outside, and I began to suspect that along with being paranoid Roy was maybe a little obsessive compulsive too. I just hoped he wasn't as whacko as my friend Elvis in Key West.

While Jessica and my uncle made coffee and puttered around the kitchen area, I wandered around the cabin. There was one large room with a sleeping loft and a kitchen area set off by an L-shaped counter. An antique wood stove set in the middle of the room chased the February chill from the air. The oak table next to the stove was well used and scarred, and the leather sofa looked well worn and comfortable.

A notebook computer and a printer sat on top of a beautiful antique desk. Alongside the desk stood an upright steel gun safe that appeared to be large enough to equip a regiment.

Bookshelves lined every wall and held an eclectic collection of reading material ranging from Homer to John D. McDonald.

Jessica appeared at my side. She reached out and ran her hand along a shelf next to the desk where about a dozen books were displayed facing outward. "Uncle Roy's a writer," she said with obvious pride.

"What does he write?" I asked.

"Mysteries." Uncle Roy walked up to where we were standing and rested a hand on Jessica's shoulder. "But my first book was a novel set in Vietnam during the final days of the war. I think it sold all of three copies."

Jessica patted the hand on her shoulder. "Uncle Roy is being modest," she said. "Every one of his books has been optioned by Hollywood."

"Not a one made into a movie though," Roy said as the background hiss of the coffeemaker sputtered into silence, filling the air with the dark aroma of coffee. Backing away from the books he added, "Come on. Let's talk."

Roy led us into the kitchen and indicated the table with a casual wave. "Have a seat. I'll get the coffee."

He filled three large ceramic mugs, set them before us and then went about laying out spoons, sugar and creamer before joining us.

"I'm not quite sure why you're here," Uncle Roy said.

Now that I was there, I wasn't quite sure either. Fish was big and tough, but I'd handled tougher. If I thought I could convince Jessica to step back and let me work the way I worked best, by myself, Fish wouldn't be a problem. And if she'd stay out of the way it would take care of our personal problems.

Before I could think of a way to explain my predicament to Roy without getting Jessica all riled up at me, she jumped in. "You know Fish Conners, Uncle Roy?"

Roy nodded. "I went to school with his daddy. Went and got himself shot dead a couple of years ago. Never could prove it, but the sheriff was convinced Fish did it. I don't doubt it. Boy inherited that mean streak from his father. People 'round here were afraid to cross him even when he was a kid."

The room was beginning to cool and Roy got up, walked over to the wood stove and stocked it with a couple of chunks of wood, then he returned to his seat.

The pleasant, fruity scent of burning apple wood filled the cabin as the logs caught and the cabin warmed almost instantly. I topped off my cup and leaned toward Roy. "So he must have been trouble before he hurt his leg?"

Roy nodded. "When he was thirteen he caught himself a baby alligator. Had that gator for about three years I guess. Raised him like a pet. Small dogs and cats began to disappear around the area. Everyone around here sort of knew it was Fish, trapping them and feeding them to the gator, but no one ever caught him."

"That's terrible," Jessica said.

Uncle Roy looked at her and twisted the hair on his beard. "Maybe, maybe not." He held up his hand before Jessica could speak again. "I'm not condoning it. But maybe folks ought to keep a better eye on their pets, not let them roam around like they do. Where was I now, oh yeah, the gator.

"Seems that one day when he was feeding that gator it up and lunged at him. There wasn't any harm done, but Fish went stomping off into the house, got his daddy's twelve gauge down off the wall and shot the critter dead.

"Not too long after that he got involved in football. I think maybe he took out all his aggressions on the other players. Then he messed up his knee and came back home meaner than ever. Heard some bad things about him, but so far he's stayed a step ahead of the cops. What's Fish got to do with getting Daddy's book back?"

I waved my hand toward my cousin. "Go ahead, Jessica."

"We think Fish might have something to do with stealing the manuscript. The other night Wes was attacked on the docks where he keeps his boat. Daddy was there and he thought it might be Fish. Then tonight we tracked him down to try talking to him. Fish attacked the both of us." Jessica tugged at a stained area of her shirt to accentuate her point.

"I was thinking I might have to go Fishing," I added. "Track the asshole down and confront him on my terms. Thought you might like to come along as backup."

Roy pushed himself away from the table. "Might be fun. But before we go any further do you even know what you're looking for, Wes?"

"I know what an illuminated manuscript is, but I can't say I've ever seen one."

"Wait here," Roy ordered, then he quick-stepped across the cabin to the desk. He opened the bottom drawer, dug around for a minute, then pulled out a file folder and brought it back to the table. He opened it, drew out a thin stack of photographs and tossed them onto the table.

Chapter 10

The photos spread apart as they slid across the table, giving me a view of half-a-dozen ornate pages. Jessica reached across the table and placed a finger on one. "That's my favorite."

It was a masterfully painted picture of the nativity with Mary dressed in a long blue robe. Her hair cascaded down her shoulders and an illuminated gold halo surrounded her head. The brown, green and red colors were as vivid as if they had been painted yesterday. The margins were decorated with hundreds of flowers and birds.

The other pages were text. Two of the pages began with large decorated letters. The calligraphy was precise and had I not known better could have been printed instead of drawn. Like the portrait page, the margins were wide and filled with flowers, birds and small animals. One page showed four humans among the flowers. They looked like little hobbits, each wearing a different color robe.

I looked up. "Any idea what it's worth?"

Roy sat back down. "I was wondering the same thing. When Daddy died I took these pictures and sent them to an antiquarian book dealer who once answered some questions for me on rare books for a novel I was working on. Guy by the name of Chet Winters.

"He called me back within a day. Said it was French, probably twelfth century. I could practically hear him drooling. He demanded to know where I got the book. Wouldn't tell me what he thought it was worth at first, but Winters was willing to hop in his car and drive down from Birmingham that day."

"And what happened after he saw the book?" I asked.

"He didn't," Roy said. "I told him it belonged to a friend who wanted to know what it was worth before he sold it. He told me the value depended on the condition of the book, if it was complete, and whether we could determine the artist and who commissioned the book. Finally he said that if all the pages were as nice looking as the ones in the photos and if the book was complete it would probably bring a couple hundred grand on up to a million bucks or better at auction. He made me promise to call him back after I talked to my friend. A week later the book was stolen."

"Could this Winters guy be behind the theft?" I asked. "It's sort of a coincidence that the book disappeared right after you talked to him."

Roy shook his head. "I don't think so. I never told him where the book was, and he's called me almost every day since then asking if my friend was ready to let him see the book."

Jessica hadn't spoken since Roy started his story, but I could tell she was dying to say something. She was fidgeting in her chair and every time Roy paused she started to lean forward. Roy must have noticed it too because he turned to her and said, "You have anything to add, Jess?" Her face clouded a little at the use of the nickname, but she ignored it.

"You didn't mention the part about why we've got to get the book back quick-like."

"What do you mean?" I asked.

Roy jumped back in. "Daddy had a special case built for the book. It was air conditioned and humidity controlled. He once told me the book would fall apart if it was out of the case for too long."

"Now you can see why we need to find the book as fast as we can," Jessica said.

Roy stood and glared down at Jessica. "When I originally told you to let this whole thing go, you promised to drop it. You never should have brought Wes into this."

Jessica jumped to her feet. "That's because after I talked to you I went to see Gran. She was afraid you'd shoot someone first and ask questions later, Uncle Roy. You know she couldn't handle you going to jail. By the way, Wes, Gran's dying to meet you. She was hurt bad when your daddy disappeared. We got to get you out there to meet her."

I felt like I was seasick and my left eye began to twitch. It wasn't bad enough that I had to contend with Jessica's advances toward me, now I had to worry about interacting with a grandmother I hadn't even known existed a few days earlier. What would I have to say to her? More importantly, how was she going to explain away the fact that she'd never tried to contact me in the past.

I took a deep breath, thought calming thoughts about sailing away from Mobile, and stood to join my newfound family. "Now what?"

"Now we go see your buddy Fish," Roy said.

"You know where we can find him?" I asked.

"Last I heard he moved into his daddy's house. It's not far from here, over in Bayou La Batre. I haven't been there in years but I don't think I'll have any trouble finding the place."

"When do you want to go see him?" I asked.

"Now's as good a time as any." Roy turned and headed across the room.

Jessica and I followed him to the gun safe. He pulled a ring of keys from his pocket, fit one into the case and opened it to reveal an extensive collection of weapons. I counted three hunting rifles, a military style rifle, a pair of Colt forty-five automatics, three smaller automatic pistols and four rather large revolvers, one of which I suspected dated back a century or more.

"We aren't playing his game though," he said. "I'm too old for fist-fighting, but I pretty much always hit what I aim at."

I shot Jessica a questioning look and she shrugged. "This is why Gran didn't want me asking Uncle Roy for help." She turned to Roy and added, "We don't want to kill Fish, Uncle Roy. We just want to talk to him."

Ignoring Jessica, Roy grabbed one of the forty-fives and handed it to me.

"You know how to use one of these?" he asked.

I ejected the clip, checked the load, and slid it back in place. "I learned to shoot on one of these. Haven't shot one in years, though."

Roy grabbed its twin and tucked it into the back of his pants. "Don't worry about it. It's just like riding a bicycle. Once you learn, you never forget."

"Kind of a cliché for a writer, isn't it?" I asked.

"I'm full of them. Have to watch myself every time I sit down to write." He started to swing the safe door shut and Jessica grabbed his arm.

"Hey. What about me?"

"You're staying right here with Dwayne." Roy slammed the door and turned the key to emphasize his point.

"Like hell I am." Jessica grabbed Roy's arm and tugged on it until he turned to face her. "I'm going. With or without a gun, with or without your permission. You know I can shoot, Uncle Roy. You taught me."

"No." Roy tried to stare her down, and then he wilted. He dropped his eyes to the floor, his huge shoulders slumped, and when Jessica held out her hand he handed over his keys.

Jessica reopened the safe, took out one of the small automatics, closed it back up and handed the keys back to Roy. Without a word she stepped around us and strutted across the floor and out into the night.

I followed Jessica, and when I got to the door I looked back at Roy. He hadn't moved from in front of the safe and seemed to be trying to figure out what had just happened. "You coming?" I asked.

Roy slid the keys into his pocket and hurried across the room to join me. "She's something else, isn't she?"

"Yes, she is," I said. I just hoped she didn't get that cocky with Fish Conners.

Chapter 11

We drove along Highway 188 for about twenty minutes before Roy ordered Jessica to slow down. He rolled down his window and leaned into the wind and there was something feral about the way he shifted his head back and forth as he studied the terrain, as if he were sniffing out a trail. We crossed a railroad track and he pulled his head back inside the car and said, "Make a right at the next turnoff and turn off your lights, then pull over."

Jessica did what Roy asked and as we climbed out of the car the first tentative drops of rain splashed on the hood. The woods around us had a damp, earthy smell, like a graveyard after a storm, and the temperature had fallen twenty degrees. The hooded sweatshirt I wore provided little comfort against the night chill that surrounded me. As I drew the hood over my head and shoved my hands into my pockets I was filled with misgivings.

Roy held up his right hand. "No talking," he said. "Sound carries in these woods." Drawing a flashlight from beneath his jacket he pointed it toward the ground in front of us. "Even a loud whisper could give us away."

Falling in line behind Jessica, I kept my eye on the bouncing flicker of Roy's flashlight as we slipped through the woods. For a moment I lost the bobbing light, only to spot it several feet to my left.

Around me I could hear the soft scrapings of animals I couldn't see. Jessica jumped and let out a whimper when an owl screeched. Wood smoke drifted along the night breeze and my nose twitched as it picked up the offensive spoor of a skunk.

The rain pelted us and the trees no longer offered protection. My clothes were soaked and the muscles in my neck and back took on a life of their own, twitching and tightening as they responded to the biting cold. Adding to my distress, the icy metal of the gun I'd earlier tucked into my belt rubbed against my hip. Overhead, a stunning lightning show jousted with the earth's surface like a barrage of anti-aircraft fire.

Preoccupied with my misery, I almost stumbled into Jessica before realizing that she and Roy had stopped at the edge of a small field. Jessica was shivering too, but Roy stood motionless, listening or waiting for a sign. I suspected that his jacket was better designed for this environment.

Roy drew us into a huddle. "Looks like our boy is home," he whispered. "There's a pickup and a Caddy in the drive and lights on in the trailer." He looked at his watch. "Nearly two a.m. I was hoping we'd catch him sleeping."

"What do we do now?" I asked. "It's your show since you seem to know the place."

"Even if Fish is awake we have the advantage of surprise," Roy whispered. "I don't want to hurt the boy unless we have to, but if we catch him unawares maybe we can scare the bejesus out of him. If he doesn't have the manuscript I'm guessing he knows where it is.

"Wes, you and I will work our way along the line of trees to the trailer. When we get there you hang back and I'll find a window to peek into—see if I can spot Fish. Jessica, you stay here as our reserve force."

"I'm not going to sit back and watch," she said. "You keep trying to protect me and I don't need protection."

"Not true, hon," Roy said. "You said it yourself. You can shoot a pistol. Up close we may have to go hand-to-hand and you're just too small to be much help. Fish is big and he's strong. I don't want to be watching out for you if it comes to a fight."

"Goddamn it Uncle Roy, I'm not going to stand out here all night waiting while you two have all of the fun. If I don't hear from one of you in a half hour, I'm coming in."

Roy gave me a light slap on the back and started forward. "Let's go. Jessica, honey, you be careful, you hear?"

Roy and I jogged along the tree line toward the rear of the trailer. As we drew even with the side of the trailer Roy picked up his pace and ducked around the corner.

I had an uneasy feeling in the pit of my stomach. Long, wavering clumps of grass dragged across my pant legs and the mud underneath sucked at my shoes and caused me to slow my pace.

I stopped and looked around. Ahead of me Roy was crouched beneath a darkened window. To my left, a small decaying barn leaned towards the woods as if it were preparing to sprint away from its sordid surroundings. From inside the barn, a dim light cast its pale glow through a doorless entry and across the yard. Dozens of castoff tires, appliances and torn plastic garbage bags littered the landscape.

I decided we needed to know if someone was in the barn. Reaching down I picked up a small stone and tossed it at Roy. He glanced back at me and I pointed to myself and then the barn. When he nodded, I made a quick dash across the junkyard obstacle course. With exaggerated care I slithered along the rough wood barn wall until I was standing alongside the doorway.

A train rattling along a nearby track sounded its horn, causing me to jump. It passed with a dull roar, and then the night became as quiet as road kill. Despite the cold I was perspiring. Forcing myself to slow down, I took a couple deep breaths and waited until I grew calm. Drawing the Colt, I held it in both hands in front of me and assumed a shooter's crouch, before creeping into the open doorway.

A single light bulb hung from the roof of the barn and cast shadows against the walls that seemed to move like crude cartoon characters. The only thing in the barn was a beautiful, restored Model T Ford resting on blocks beneath the light.

Outside, rain pelted the barn. Inside, wide rivulets of water poured through what was left of the roof, turning the dirt floor into a giant caldron of mud.

I stood and was about to turn back into the night when something heavy slammed into my head.

***

Someone called my name from a distance. The voice sounded urgent and became louder as my mind began to focus. I was lying with the right side of my face pressed against the muddy floor of the barn. My hands were tied behind my back and my feet were bound together. The mud smelled of age-old straw and bird dung, and was almost as disagreeable as the damp, frigid outside air that filtered in through a thousand cracks and missing boards.

"Wes, can you hear me?" the voice called again. I turned my head, groaned as a sliver of pain pierced my brain, and saw my cousin and Roy lying bound beside me.

"Jessica." I called out. "Roy."

"I'm okay," Jessica said. "But Uncle Roy hasn't moved since they brought me in here. I'm worried, Wes."

As I pulled and twisted my bindings, I willed myself to stop shivering. It didn't work. "How did you get caught?" I asked.

"I did something really stupid. When you and Uncle Roy didn't show, I snuck up to the trailer but there wasn't anyone there. I assumed you found it empty too and so I called out. I didn't even have my gun out of my pocket when Fish and that Rusty guy you know showed up."

"Are you sure it was Rusty?"

"Absolutely," she said. "The son of a bitch tied me up and he wasn't very gentle about it."

"I wondered how Fish knew how to find me," I said. "Or that I was interested in the manuscript for that matter. I told everything to Rusty and he must have relayed it to Fish. I don't understand it though. I was told Rusty had a lot of money."

"Had is the operative word there, Wes. I had a lot of money."

I turned my head as Rusty entered the barn followed by Fish Conners.

"So this is all about making a quick buck?" I asked.

"Pretty much," Rusty said. He turned his head, spit on the ground and walked over to where I lay. "I was self-employed when Elaine took sick and we didn't have insurance. It took most of our savings just to pay her hospital bills."

"How did you know about the manuscript?" I asked.

"After your Granddaddy died I stopped by to offer Fran my condolences. She showed me the book and told me she was going to try to return it to the original owner. I suggested she contact Sam Quinlin. He's an old schoolmate of Fish's. I've been around enough to know the book was worth some money, but I didn't know how much until Quinlin started researching the damn thing. I figured that if Fran was going to give it away, it might as well be mine. I offered Quinlin a cut but he got all righteous on me so he had to be dealt with."

"You're a pig," Jessica said. "Gran trusted you."

"The way Fran felt about that book, I didn't figure she'd try too hard to get it back from us. Now the only question is what to do with the three of you."

"You could just let us go," I suggested without much hope. "We'll forget any of this happened. You can keep the damn book."

"It's a little too late for that," Rusty said. "The three of you know about Quinlin and me. Can't leave any witnesses."

Roy let out a groan and tried to sit up. "You don't have to hurt Jessica," he said.

Rusty spit on the muddy floor by his feet. "I wish I could let y'all go. But truthfully, Roy, she's too damn stubborn for her own good. She wouldn't rest until she brought me down."

"You got that right," Jessica said.

"See what I mean." Rusty turned toward Fish. "Wait until I'm out of here and have a chance to get home before you take care of them. I don't want to be anywhere near here. Understand?"

"You bastard!" Jessica gave a sudden heave to her body, rolled across my legs and lashed out with her tied feet. She connected with Rusty's right leg causing him to lose his balance and fall to the floor.

Fish was on her in an instant. Grabbing her by the hair he gave it a vicious twist and dragged her to her feet. She spit in his face and he cursed and tossed her across the barn where she landed with a dull thud. I cringed as she cried out in pain, but there was nothing I could do.

Rusty climbed to his feet and headed out the door without looking back at us. "She's all yours, Fish. Why don't you give the little bitch an introduction to hell before you kill her?"

"Rusty, wait," I said, but he continued walking until he disappeared into the night. A moment later I heard his car start and drive away.

"Let us go, Fish," Roy said. He was moving about, straining at his bonds. "You know your Daddy wouldn't want you to hurt no woman."

"You don't know what Daddy was like," Fish said. "When I was twelve I watched him rape two colored whores. Couldn't have been much older than me. When he finished with 'em he made me help feed 'em to the gators. Bastard promised me I'd be next if I ever told anyone." Fish gave a quick glance over his shoulder as if he expected his long dead father to step out of the dark, then he moved over to where Jessica lay.

"I'll leave you two out here so you can think about what I'm gonna do to this here girl. Maybe if you're lucky you'll freeze to death before I get back."

Slipping a knife from his pocket Fish opened it with a flick of his wrist and reached down to slice the ropes from her legs. He dragged Jessica to her feet and when she tried to pull away he gave her a sharp clap across the side of her head. Without another glance our way he headed toward the door of the barn, half leading, half dragging Jessica behind him.

Roy was still struggling with his bindings.

"Save your energy," I said. "Maybe if we back up to each other one of us can untie the other."

It took several minutes to swing our bodies around and back into place. The mud numbed my fingers, and after a few unsuccessful minutes I stopped.

"Fish knows how to tie a knot," I said. "I'm not having any luck, want to give it a try?"

"I can't even feel my hands right now." I could hear the desperation in Roy's voice and knew he was as afraid for Jessica as I was. I took another look around the barn, twisted onto my side, and began rolling toward the Model T. Icy needles of pain shot through my arms and legs and I wondered if I'd ever see Jessica again.

I was encapsulated with mud that smelled like rat shit and molting feathers. It cleared my sinuses and made me nauseous. Easing to a stop against one of the tires, I allowed myself a moment to catch my breath while I studied the area around the car. I was hoping to find a toolbox, a knife, anything that would help cut me free. Nothing. As an afterthought I rolled under the carriage of the car where I found an edged piece of metal. I then arched my body until my hands rested against the rough steel.

I'm not sure what was worse, the chips of flesh I shaved from my hands as I moved the ropes across the metal piece, or the biting strain on my back from trying to reach the makeshift cutting tool. After what seemed like an hour the bindings parted, and I lay on my stomach until my dead hands tickled back to life.

My feet threatened to slide out from beneath me as I skated across the muddied floor to where Roy lay. Again, I fumbled unsuccessfully with his knots. "Just leave me," he said. "Who knows what that animal is doing to Jessica? Go see if you can help her."

I sprang to my feet and was almost to the door when two shots rang out. I doubled my speed and burst into the night in time to see Fish Conners climb into his car and take off down the drive, spinning his tires as he hit the road.

When I reached the trailer I hesitated for a moment before tearing open the door, afraid of what I'd find, hoping against hope that I was wrong.

The place was a pigsty. The sink was piled with dirty dishes. Crusted pots and pans filled the stove. In the center of the kitchen a filthy folding table held an army of empty beer cans and a large ashtray overflowing with half smoked joints and cigar butts. I gagged at the stench of bacon grease, sour milk, stale tobacco, and pot.

Someone had removed the carpet from the living room floor leaving dark patches of glue. The two chairs and sofa were torn and faded, and covered with newspapers, CD jackets and videotapes.

In the corner, a sixty-inch projection TV was tuned to a talk show whose host I didn't recognize. The volume was turned down so low that the cheering audience sounded almost like the ocean's surf heard through a giant conch shell. The only other sound in the trailer was the ticking of an old clock hanging over the sofa.

The door to the bedroom was ajar and by the time I was halfway across the living room I could see that the bed was empty. Stepping through the doorway, my heart went cold as my gaze followed a thin trail of blood that ran from the pillow, across the dingy sheets, and along the floorboards.

Chapter 12

made a quick spin and raced back through the trailer, only to be confronted at the doorway by my cousin. Her blouse was ripped open. Dried blood stained her lips, neck and bra, and there was a haunted glaze in her eyes.

"I thought you were dead," I said.

It took a moment but her eyes cleared and a smile threatened to replace the frown on her face. "I bit the son of a bitch's finger through to the bone. I tried my best to bite the damn thing off, but the bone just wouldn't give."

"We heard gunshots and I saw Fish drive off."

Jessica started laughing, a soft gurgle that grew to a squawk. Giant sobs followed, and tears flowed down her face as she threw herself against my chest and clutched at me.

Something akin to liquid fire rushed through my veins. I wanted to hold her close and kiss away her tears, but that was a path I could never allow myself to follow. They say blood is thicker than water, and as far as I was concerned that blood was a dense social wall that I could never breach.

So I held her at arm's length and spoke soothing, if meaningless words as I willed her anguish away.

"We need to get moving," I said. "Fish or Rusty might come back at any time. Wait here for a minute while I find a knife or something to cut Roy loose."

She nodded, but she didn't move away from me so I backed further into the kitchen, reached over, and tore out a drawer. Seeing only towels I let it crash to the floor and moved over to the next one. In the third drawer I found what I was looking for.

Not only was there a nice folding Buck knife, but all three of our pistols were tucked under a stained dishrag. I checked each gun and found that they were still loaded. Slipping the knife into my pocket, I turned back to Jessica.

Forcing the nine-millimeter into her right hand, I slid one of the forty-fives into my waistband, and then racked a bullet into the chamber of the other. Taking Jessica by the elbow, I guided her from the trailer and out to the barn. As we made our way across the lot, she told me what had happened.

"He kept telling me how much I was going to like his 'Big Willie.' It was disgusting." As she talked, she grabbed my arm and held it as if she were afraid I might disappear.

"He cut me loose when we got to the bedroom," she continued. "He was trying to retie my arms to the bedpost when I got hold of his finger. God, did he let out a scream."

"So that's where all the blood came from?" I asked.

"Yup. He tried shaking me off but I just clamped down on the finger. It was the hardest thing I've ever done in my life, but I wasn't going to give in without a fight.

"That's when he cuffed me across the ear and shook me off. I rolled off the bed and took off like a coon running from a hungry gator. I don't know where the gun came from, but Fish fired a couple times as I headed for the trees. I hid until I saw his car pull away. I figure he was headed to a hospital. I hope he loses the damn finger."

Roy had managed to roll several feet outside the barn entrance. A thick blanket of mud and straw covered his entire body and he looked like a boar in pig heaven.

"Thank God," Roy said when he saw Jessica. "I was worried half to death about you."

"What, you weren't concerned about me?" I asked. I bent down and began sawing at his ropes with the Buck knife.

"I figured you could handle yourself," he said.

The blade was sharp and I quickly hacked him loose. Roy rubbed his hands together and groaned as the blood began circulating. "Where's that bastard, Fish? I'm going to kill the son of a bitch with my bare hands. Soon as I can use them again, that is."

"Maybe it's time to go to the police," I said, as Jessica and I helped Roy to his feet.

"We can't do that," Jessica said.

"Why not?" I asked.

"Because Ma wouldn't want Daddy exposed as a thief," Roy chipped in. "She'd rather the manuscript stay stolen than have that happen. Now what the hell happened at the trailer?"

Jessica filled him in and then we headed back to the car.

"I knew I should have made you stay at my place," Roy said as we tramped along behind him.

"Like that was going to happen," Jessica said.

Roy grabbed her by the arm and dragged her to a stop. "You're out of this as of right now."

"If it wasn't for me biting Fish's finger near off and sending him scurrying away, we'd all be dead," she said.

"She's right, you know," I said.

"Whose side are you on, anyway?" Roy asked.

"I'm not on anyone's side," I said. "Do you really think you can keep her out of this? At least if she's with us we can keep an eye on her. Otherwise she's going to do whatever she wants and she's liable to get herself killed."

Jessica tore her arm from Roy's grip and started walking. "Finding the book was my idea in the first place and I'm not going to sit by and let the two of you have all the fun."

"Yeah, this is my definition of fun," I muttered as we trudged back through the woods. If Jessica heard me, she ignored the comment.

When we reached the car Jessica held out her keys and asked, "Will you drive, Wes?"

I took the keys and we climbed into the car, Jessica and Roy in the back. As we headed back to Roy's cabin, my eyes searched every cutoff and parking area for signs of Fish or Rusty. I was struck by the realization that I was becoming quite fond of my cousin.

We made it back to the cabin without further incident. The sky was making its morning shift from black to gray as we coasted to a stop alongside Roy's beat up truck. "Jessica, you're staying with me," he said. "Wes, you're welcome too. I've got an air mattress we can set up on the floor if you'd like."

"I'll pass. I want to get back to the marina. I need to check on the boat and I'd rather sleep in my own bed than on the floor."

"All right," Roy said. "Take Jessica's car and I'll bring her on out to the marina later today to pick it up. We can have dinner and discuss our plans."

"Maybe we should come along," Jessica said. "What if they're waiting for you?"

I shook my head. "Judging by the blood on the floor I suspect Fish has gone off to lick his wounds and maybe get a couple of stitches. But if you don't mind, Roy, I'll hang onto the gun for a few days."

Roy gave me a quick pat on the shoulder. "Keep the gun until this is all over, but I'm surprised you don't have one of your own on board."

"When I sailed up the coast from Key West I didn't expect to be out playing cowboys and Indians."

"I don't think any of us expected things to get this messy," Roy said. "Why don't we plan on meeting out at the marina around four-thirty?"

The two of them climbed out of the car and I shifted into gear and began to creep away. Roy said something I couldn't make out, so I stopped and rolled down the window. "What's that?"

"Jessica's right, Wes. You need to be careful. They may not act at all like we expect."

"I'll keep an eye out."

I left the window open and let the cold air brush away my tiredness and clear my mind. It was a long trip back to the marina and the last thing I needed was to fall asleep at the wheel.

As I drove, my thoughts ran the gauntlet from despair to anger, and after awhile I was overcome with a strange exhilaration that bordered on depression.

All I'd wanted when I sailed into Mobile Bay was to find out why I'd never heard from my father or his side of the family. I'd never envisioned miserable cold nights without sleep, gunfights, or the developing closeness I felt toward Jessica.

When I got to the marina I had to drag my body from the car. Letting out a groan I hunched my shoulders against the frosty breeze that was winding its way off Mobile Bay and along the Dog River. I slogged my way across the parking lot and over to the round table where I found Cathy sprawled out across two chairs. She was holding a cigarette in one hand and a near empty bottle of Captain Morgan in the other.

She didn't appear to have heard me walk up to the table and I wondered if I should leave her alone. Next to where she was seated, cigarette butts lined the edge of the table like little white fence posts. As I watched, she stubbed out her current butt and placed it in the row before lighting another.

I cleared my throat. "I didn't know you smoked."

"Quit six years ago." She looked up at me and took a swig of her rum.

Her eyes were dull, her face slack from the liquor, and in the damning half-light she appeared old and worn. I moved around the table and sat down across from her, uninvited, and asked, "Is something wrong?"

"No, Wes. I always sit outside all night smoking and drinking and freezing my ass off."

I leaned forward. "Want to talk about it?"

She shook her head no. "Men are all bastards."

"All of us?" I asked, as she lined up another cigarette and took another sip of rum.

"Last night I got a call from Rob, my ex-husband. The cops are dropping all the charges against him. He's driving down to see me today."

"Is that good or bad?"

"Well it ain't good." She took a hefty swig from the bottle. Her body gave the impression that it was swaying in the wind, and for a moment I thought she was going to pass out. Instead, she folded her upper body across the table and let out a fetid trace of steam as her warm breath crossed the icy air. "I left Wisconsin to get away from the prick."

I leaned away from the sour scent that radiated from her. "I thought you were still in love with him?"

"I am?" She gave me a confused look that turned to belligerence. "I mean I am! I was. I don't know. That was before you and me and all that shit. I always seem to want what I can't have and not want what I can."

She waved the bottle and gave me a hideous grin. "I'm one seriously messed up chick, Wes. Want some advice from a woman who's been through a thing or two?"

"Sure," I said.

"Get on your frigging boat and run as fast and far from this crazy hick state as you can. I've seen the way that cousin of yours looks at you. She's trouble, Wes."

She took one more drink, slammed the bottle onto the table so hard I was afraid it might shatter, and then laid her head onto her arms and started snoring.

Leaving her asleep out in the cold was not a consideration. I didn't dare take her to my boat. Rusty or Fish might show up, or worse yet, Jessica. I was too tired to deal with that situation right now.

That left Cathy's boat, and I wasn't too sure I could carry her all the way down to the far side of the marina where it was docked. I looked around, took a sip of rum for warmth, and then walked over to the office. I grabbed the wheeled dock cart that was used as a general carryall around the marina and pushed it to where Cathy lay.

I hadn't slept much in the last twenty-four hours and it was a real workout getting her into the cart. After a bit of struggling and a tuck here, a tuck there, I was ready to move her. The trip was easier than carrying her, but in several places the unevenness of the dock almost caused me to tip her into the river.

I struggled for ten minutes before we reached her houseboat and I was glad to see it was unlocked. In fact, the sliding glass door was wide open. The cool crisp air battled a tiny electric space heater, and the cold was winning.

I half carried, half dragged Cathy into the boat and laid her onto her bed. She opened her eyes as I placed her on the mattress, looked at me as if I weren't there, and then rolled over onto her side and started snoring again.

I slipped off her shoes, pulled a blanket up around her shoulders, and looked around the boat to make sure everything was all right before heading back to the round table area, dragging the cart behind me like a stubborn mule.

Chapter 13

Back at my boat the first thing I did was tuck the forty-five under the settee cushion. Then I grabbed my bathroom kit, some clean clothes, and a towel before heading down to the boaters' showers. I lathered up, turned the water as hot as I could stand it, and basked under the steamy flow for a good twenty minutes. While I shaved, I studied my face in the mirror. I wasn't happy with what I saw. To make matters worse, the cuts were beginning to sting and itch, and the bruises felt as if they were forming bruises on top of bruises.

When I stepped out into the brisk morning air I headed over to the round table. I knew I wouldn't be alone for long.

Within minutes Cajun Bob, Phil and Renee Hamlin, and Too Tall Bob joined me. Too Tall, a six-foot, six-inch tall, retired fisherman, didn't own a boat. However, he liked the ambiance around the marina and showed up every morning for coffee.

"Any of you guys seen Rusty?" I asked, as Houseboat Barbie hurried up the dock. She was built like an Amazon version of Dolly Pardon and worked the store in the early morning. Barbie had married and buried two octogenarians by the time she was forty. According to

Renee, Barbie was now broke, had a huge mortgage on her houseboat, and was desperately searching for octogenarian number three.

Ignoring my question, Phil said, "You look like shit, Wes."

"Be nice, Phil." Renee looked at me over the top rim of her glasses. "You know, you have looked better, Wes. A lover's spat?"

"Lover's spat hell." Cajun Jeff squinted, and sucked in his bottom lip. "You look like you've been whooped with an ugly stick. Some of those cuts are pretty deep. Maybe you should see a doctor."

"I had a little too much to drink last night and I tripped," I said, eager to change the subject.

"On someone's fist," Phil mumbled under his breath.

"About Rusty," I said.

"I couldn't sleep last night," Houseboat Barbie said. "I was reading an old John D. McDonald book, one of those Travis McGee ones, *Nightmare in Pink*, I think. I'm terrible with titles. Don't know what I'm reading half the time.

"Anyway, it was around four this morning. Rusty was with some guy I didn't recognize. They were right under that big light by Rusty's boat and let me tell you, this one threw a shadow like one of those Clydesdale horses, if you know what I mean. They were casting off the dock lines and seemed to be in a pretty big hurry. I thought maybe they were heading out on a fishing trip, but instead of motoring out onto the bay, they turned up-river. Toward Rusty's place."

"You know where Rusty lives up there?" I asked.

"Somewhere along Rabbit Creek," Barbie said. "I can get you his phone number out of the marina files if you want."

I shook my head and backed away. "That's okay," I said. "It's not that important. I'm sure I'll be seeing him in the next day or so. Look guys. I'm getting too old for this late night shit. I'm going to get some shut eye."

"If I see Rusty, I'll tell him you were looking for him," Barbie said.

"No!" I said. Cajun Bob threw me a questioning look and I added, "I don't want him coming down and waking me up. I'll catch him later."

***

It was four p.m. when my phone woke me. I let it go to voicemail as I crawled out of bed. When I was dressed I picked it up, punched in the code for my messages and listened as Jessica informed me that she and Roy would be out to the marina in about an hour. I made myself a pot of coffee, sat on the settee and turned on the Weather Channel.

After watching the local report I pulled on my last clean and dry hooded sweatshirt, grabbed my jacket and slipped on a pair of heavy socks with my hiking boots. No more under dressing for me, I thought as I headed out.

Roy and Jessica hadn't arrived when I got to the parking lot, so I made my way up the back dock to Cathy's slip where I bent forward and knocked on the side of her boat. Nothing. I knocked again, this time with more enthusiasm.

Again my effort was met with silence.

I rapped one more time, a little harder, and was rewarded with an echoing curse. The boat rocked from side to side as though a giant troll was making its way along the inside corridors of the vessel. When the door flew open I realized my analogy wasn't far off.

Cathy wore the same jeans and shirt she had on when I put her to bed early that morning. Her hair was twisted, knotted and coiled. Dried spittle flecked her lips and chin and she appeared to have a serious case of pinkeye.

I gave her my brightest smile. "How you doing?"

"You got me out of bed to ask me a stupid question like that? How do you think I'm doing?"

"I was hoping you felt better than you look."

"You don't look like you stepped out of GQ yourself," she said.

I reached up and touched my face and winced when I moved my fingers across the largest cut. "No, I don't. I dropped by to see if you needed anything."

"Judging from your reaction when you saw me, I suspect a shower wouldn't hurt."

Her voice lightened when she said it and that's when I knew she was going to be all right. "You're on your own there," I said. "I was thinking more in terms of food or drink."

"I may never eat or drink again," she said. "I think I'm going to clean up a little, then climb right back into bed."

"You have my number," I said. "Call if you need anything. If I'm not around leave a message and I'll come over as soon as I can."

"Wes," she called out as I started down the dock. "Thanks for everything. Last night. Just stopping to check on me. You know."

"Sure." Neither of us seemed to have anything else to say so I waited until she closed the door and continued on down the dock.

As I reached the parking lot Roy's old truck came rumbling in. He pulled up next to where I'd left Jessica's car and he and Jessica climbed out and joined me.

They were dressed for an evening out. Roy wore his hair tied back, khaki Dockers and a green sweater that was a little too bright and a little too shaggy for my tastes.

"Jessica convinced me that tonight should be just a nice night out," Roy said. "We haven't spent any time talking about anything but that damn book."

"Are you saying you want to let the book go?" I asked.

He must have heard the surprise in my voice because he snapped back his answer. "I'm not letting Rusty or Fish get away with the book, Wes."

"Which brings me back to the question—why don't we go to the cops?" I asked.

"Ma's afraid it will hurt Daddy's reputation," Roy said. "He was a minister at the church they went to, and if it comes out that he stole the book in the first place, people will talk."

"You never did explain exactly how he got the manuscript," I said.

"I told you," Jessica chimed in. "He took it off a dead German's body at the end of the war."

I turned my attention to Jessica. She looked good in her hip hugging beige slacks and tight yellow sweater. The matching yellow headband that swept her hair back and out of the way gave her a playful look. She was hot and it was all I could do to keep from drooling. I knew right then that when we sat down to eat I had to keep the table between us.

"A lot of soldiers brought souvenirs back at the end of the war," I said. "I believe all they had to do was fill out some paperwork."

"You're talking flags and swords," Roy said. "This is a piece of rare art, probably stolen from a monastery or a museum. It's worth a lot of money. Besides, Ma just can't live with the idea of what people will say. Her reason doesn't have to make sense, it's the way she feels, and if we bring in the police word's bound to get out. Wes, you don't even know Ma, so if you want to back out, I'll understand."

"Well I won't," Jessica said.

"I didn't say anything about backing out. I just wanted to clarify things."

"Good." Jessica took each of us by the arm and guided us up the stairs to the marina restaurant. "Enough shop talk. Wes, I want to hear a little about your life before Mobile and how you came to live on a sailboat."

And so we ate burgers and fries. We laughed a little and I told them about my mother, the family detective business, and my living on a boat. Roy talked about his parents, and a little about my father.

Roy didn't have a whole lot to say. He told me my father had played baseball for his high school team and that back then Roy had been jealous of his little brother because the girls seemed to love him. He also told me that my father often talked about not fitting in, despite his popularity.

While I dwelled on what I'd learned, Jessica leaned toward me. "Gran would love to meet you. She'd like to know what you're like," she said.

A synapse misfired in my brain, a dark cloud enveloped me, and my mood took a downward spiral. It was depression à la mode for dessert.

"She should have thought about that when I was growing up. I know my mother contacted her, but I never heard from her. Not a card or a call in thirty years. She didn't seem very interested in learning about me then."

Roy pushed his plate away. "Ma's a good woman caught up in a bad situation," he said. "To be fair, your ma asked her to stay out of your life."

"How convenient," I said.

"It's eating at her big-time. And it's much worse since you got here," Jessica added.

I stood, took two twenties from my pocket and threw them on the table. "Dinner's on me," I said, and then I turned and walked out of the restaurant.

Outside, the crisp breeze carried the scent of grilled meats and hickory. All I wanted was to go back to my boat and lie down. A light pressure on my arm told me that Jessica had moved up alongside of me.

"Are you all right?"

"Call it a case of Dog River Blues," I said. "I just don't think I'm ready to meet a grandmother I didn't even know existed a month ago. I haven't come to grips with meeting you and Roy yet." Or that kiss you laid on me, I thought.

I was saved from any more tawdry thoughts when Roy joined us. As we walked down to the parking lot he said, "Why don't we concentrate on getting the manuscript back? After that you can decide what you want to do about meeting Ma."

"He's just being pig-headed," Jessica said. "And we're the ones who are gonna have to tell Gran he won't see her. She's eighty years old, Wes, and she doesn't need any more disappointment in her life."

I felt my face go red. Maybe she was right, but I couldn't change my feelings.

"I don't need this shit." I felt the venom in my voice as I added, "I'd have been better off if I'd stayed away from Mobile."

Jessica threw her shoulders back and stalked off to her car. As she walked she searched her purse, and when it dawned on her that I still had her keys she stomped back to where we stood and held out her hand without looking at me.

I felt worn and beaten as I held out Jessica's keys. "Maybe we should just let Rusty keep the damn thing."

"Right, just quit." Jessica snapped the keys from my hand. "Why didn't you damn Yankees do that back during the War of Northern Aggression, when it would have mattered."

Roy and I stood there, watching as she jumped into her car and sped away. "She's got a temper," he said.

I stared after my cousin in amazement. "Did she really bring up the Civil War?" I asked.

Roy rested his hand on my shoulder and gave it a squeeze. "Down here some of us are still fighting the war. We don't even refer to it as the Civil War. To us, there was only one war. By the way, you know what they say the difference between a Yankee and a damn Yankee is, don't you?"

"I don't think I want to hear this," I said.

Roy laughed. "A Yankee comes down here in the winter, spends a lot of money, and then goes back north for the summer. A damn Yankee comes down here and stays."

The dark veil began to lift as I realized that I liked these Southern relatives of mine after all. I wasn't quite sure what it was that made me hesitate about meeting my grandmother.

"You can tell Jessica that I'm not going to back out," I said.

Roy slapped me on the shoulder. "Never thought you were," Roy said.

"I think we're going to have to visit Rusty's house next," I said.

"Any idea where he lives?" he asked.

We started walking towards Roy's truck and I debated how much to tell him. I was planning on making a reconnaissance visit that evening to look for Rusty's house and boat. I didn't think having him or Jessica along would help much. In fact, more than one person wandering around might prove to be a hindrance.

We stopped at Roy's truck. "I know he lives up river," I said. "I'll get back to you when I have more information."

Roy gave me a quizzical look. "You're not going to do anything stupid, are you?"

"Not a chance." I didn't add that I was going to actually take my dinghy out to Rusty's place. I wanted to keep Jessica out of harm's way again. Since Roy had admitted that he couldn't say no to her, I wasn't about to tell him my plans for the night.

"I think we need to go see Rusty tomorrow night," Roy said.

I nodded. "I'll ask around and find out exactly where he lives."

"All right," Roy got in his truck and started it. He raised his voice so that he could be heard above the rattle of the engine. "I'll call you tomorrow and set up a time."

I nodded and watched as he backed up the truck and drove away, then headed back to my boat. At least the clouds were covering the moon. It looked like a perfect night to pay Rusty a visit.

Chapter 14

It took three pulls of the cord to get the outboard started, and I gave the engine a little gas to make sure it wasn't going to quit on me. Satisfied, I shoved the dinghy away from the boat and headed up the river toward Rabbit Creek.

I love boating at night. It's a paradox. Sound travels farther in the still air. Every little splash has an impact on your psyche. The air smells fresher, lights seem brighter, but every time you hear a motor nearby, tension builds along your nerve endings and questions form in your mind. Could that motor belong to a boat driven by a drunk? Will someone not see you in the night darkness? Danger, be it real or imagined, reigns supreme in the pooling shadows.

I cut the engine as I turned into Rabbit Creek. Up ahead I saw Rusty's boat tied to a dock behind a house. Shutting off the navigation lights I drifted with the current and slid the oars into the water. Above, the moon threatened to burst from its cloud cover.

There were no lights on the dock or the boat, although as I glided by I noticed light pouring from every window in the house up the hill from the creek.

Perhaps fifty feet beyond his trawler a large clump of bushes hung out over the water. I tied the dinghy to a large branch and considered my options.

I hadn't brought the gun and after what had happened at Fish's place I wasn't about to go sulking around by myself. I could call Roy, but I wanted to keep Jessica out of the action. I wasn't sure I could count on him to tell her no. I decided to return to my boat and talk to Roy the next day.

As I made my way back to the marina, the moon rolled out from behind one of the few remaining clouds. Despite the clearing sky, the air was filled with the rich, moist smell of a pending storm. Somewhere, a heron screeched, and the distant wail of an ambulance pierced the night.

By the time I got to my boat I was having trouble keeping my eyes open. The last few nights had been filled with anything but sleep. With leaden arms I tied off the dinghy and dragged myself up and onto my boat.

Stepping into the cabin I switched on the lights. Like a stubborn nightmare, a large shadow was delivered from the darkness, and I found myself looking down the malignant barrel of Roy's Colt forty-five.

"About time you got here," Fish Conners said, smiling up at me from the starboard settee. Three empty beer bottles lay on the floor beside him and the place had been ransacked. He was holding a bottle of Miller Lite in his left hand and as he tilted it up to take a swig I noticed that his pinky was heavily bandaged.

"Nice to see you made yourself comfortable," I said, as I considered what to do.

I didn't like my options, but I was preparing to jump back into the cockpit when Fish threw the bottle to the floor and sprang to his feet.

"Hey smart ass," he said, as if reading my mind. "Don't even think about it. I can't miss at this distance, even if I close my eyes. I guarantee you that I'll be gone before anyone can get down here to investigate, and you'll be stone dead."

Ever the realist, I raised my hands. "So now what?"

Fish made a circular motion with the gun. "Rusty wants to talk to you. My truck's in the lot, why don't you lead the way. And remember, I won't think twice about shooting you."

"I find it hard to believe he wants to talk." I said. "Are you sure he doesn't want to kill me?"

Fish shrugged. "He said he wants to talk. If he wanted you dead he would have told me to kill you. He didn't. Now let's go or I might shoot you just for the hell of it."

It was late, the marina was deserted and I had nowhere to run and no one to turn to for help. He made another waving motion with the gun, and I led the way down to the parking lot and his truck.

"Here." Fish held out his keys. "You drive. And remember I don't have a problem with shooting you. Get in on my side and slide over so I can keep an eye on you."

Fish pushed the Colt against my ribs and followed me into the cab of the truck. He was breathing hard and had a ripe, reptilian smell about him that I found repugnant.

My mind shifted from the gun, to the task at hand, as I fit the key in the ignition. When I reached over to turn up the heater, he poked me with the gun and said, "No tricks."

"I just want a little heat," I said.

He twisted the barrel of the gun into my ribs and when I groaned he said, "Take a right on D.I.P., and then a right at the next light. We'll be there in two minutes."

His time estimate wasn't far off. When I pulled the car to a stop behind Rusty's Cadillac, Fish once again dug the gun into my side. "Slide out after me," he said. "Then go over to the door. It'll be unlocked. Walk right in and take a seat."

Fish followed me into the house, never moving far from my side. There was no opportunity to escape. I took a deep breath, willed my mind to stay clear, and opened the door. As I crossed the room I couldn't help but notice the furniture marks pressed into the plush carpet. I was studying one of those marks, wondering where the table that had rested there had gone, when Rusty walked in.

"Have a seat, Wes," he said.

I hesitated and he sauntered over to Fish. Holding out his hand, he waited until Fish handed it to him, then he turned to face me.

"I said sit down."

The casual way Rusty handled the forty-five suggested that it wasn't the first time he'd held a handgun. I sat and Fish left the room.

Rusty brushed his foot over the furniture print I'd been examining. "Louis the Fourteenth," he said. "That table was one of my most prized possessions."

He made a panoramic gesture with the pistol and added, "All my antiques are gone now. I've had to sell them one by one just to live. Let me tell you something, Wes. Nobody wants to make a drastic change in lifestyle, but it's even harder when you're sixty-eight years old. I see this manuscript as the means to get my lifestyle back for the few years I have left."

"I don't know why you're telling me all of this."

He took a seat opposite me. He was dressed in dark slacks, a white shirt, and had combed his hair over to cover his bald spot. With practiced ease he straightened his pant leg, placed his right leg over his left knee, and then nestled the pistol, still clenched in his right hand, into his lap.

"I'm prepared to make you an offer. Ten thousand dollars if you keep your kin folk out of my hair for the next day or two."

"Why would I do that?"

"They're strangers to you, boy. You didn't know them a week ago. None of this concerns you."

"Hypothetically speaking, let's say I accept your offer. You're prepared to hand me ten thousand in cash—tonight?"

"Look around. I think it's pretty clear I don't have that kind of cash lying around. Once we sell the book I'll give you your cut."

"I'm not sure I can stop Jessica. She's a strong minded woman."

He pointed the gun at me. "Then I guess I'll have to reconsider my offer."

"No," I said. "On second thought I'm sure I can keep her out of your way."

Rusty shook his head and tapped the barrel of the gun against his leg. "You don't sound very convincing, Wes."

I sprang to my feet and Rusty lifted the Colt and pointed it at my chest. Despite the weight of the gun, his arm never wavered, even when he heaved himself up from the chair. I began to perspire.

"I'd rather not shoot you right here, Wes. Blood's a bitch to get out of carpet. Then again, it might be cheaper to replace it."

"You don't need to shoot me." My knees felt loose and I was afraid they might give out at any moment. I had no doubt that Rusty would kill me without a second thought.

"Sit back down," he said.

I plopped backward into the cushions and gripped the armrests, as if that action might offer me a dollop of protection.

"Fish, get in here," Rusty called out. There was no answer, so he raised his voice and tried again. This time Fish shouted something indecipherable from the other room. In a minute, he entered the room carrying a thick, half eaten sandwich in one hand and a beer in the other. At the sight of the sandwich my stomach began to rumble, and I was shocked to discover that I was hungry.

"I don't suppose you have one of those for me?" I asked.

"I admire a man who can think about eating while knowing he's going to die," Rusty said, just before he swiped the side of my head with the pistol.

Dog River Blues

Chapter 15

The blow stunned me and I slid off the chair. Fish rushed across the room, grabbed the collar of my shirt, and manhandled me to my feet. At the same time Rusty reached down and plucked my phone from its holster.

"You won't need this." Rusty jabbed the gun into my ribs. "Fish, there's some rope in the kitchen drawer next to the fridge. Let's get Wes here tied up. Then I think we need to make a trip to the bayou."

"I know just the place," Fish said.

It was as if I'd traded my brain for a gyroscope and my knees began to buckle. When Fish released me I felt like I was on the deck of a boat in the middle of a storm. I would have fallen if Rusty hadn't reached out and gripped my elbow.

"I'm too old to carry you," Rusty said. "You can walk to the bedroom or I can have Fish drag you. It's the open doorway up ahead and to your right."

"What difference does it make? You're going to kill me either way."

"Not true. We're going to take you somewhere and dump you. By the time you make your way out the book will be gone and we can stop this nonsense."

We both knew he was lying, but I figured as long as I was alive I had a chance of escaping. I took a tentative step, then another. Rusty released my arm and I tottered toward the door he'd indicated.

The room reeked of old cigarette smoke and mildew. The draperies looked expensive, but even to my untrained eye appeared outdated and dingy. Once again, the most noticeable feature of the room was the lack of furniture. There was a bed with a blue and pink bedspread, and an end table with a light sitting on it.

Rusty nudged me toward the bed with the gun.

"Face down on the bed," he said. "Hands behind your back."

As I climbed onto the bed Fish entered the room. He held a length of rope in one hand and a knife in the other. With a nod from Rusty he moved over to the bed and began tying my hands behind my back. He then tied my legs and the two of them left the room, closing the door behind them.

The bedspread was so stiff that it felt like a Brillo pad rubbing against the side of my face. I counted to ten to make sure no one was going to walk back into the room, and then I went to work on my bindings.

My struggles bore no fruit. All I got for my efforts were rope-burned wrists, and a vicious pounding in my head. A wave of nausea washed over me that was so severe I thought I'd pass out. I was on the verge of losing the battle to stay alert, when the door opened and Rusty walked in.

"Wes. I'm sorry about all this. I like you, and I wish we could have come to some sort of an agreement."

"We could reopen negotiations." My words echoed in my head and I was having trouble understanding what he was saying.

Rusty studied my face, and then he pursed his lips and shook his head. "It's not going to happen. All I can promise is that if you don't act up, don't make things hard for Fish and myself, I'll make sure he goes easy on you."

"Come on Rusty." I fought to deliver the right words, to clear my mind. "Why don't you at least say it like it is? You're going to murder me."

He nodded. "I did try to avoid that option."

"Not very hard," I said.

"Quite the contrary." He sat on the edge of the bed, reached out, and for a moment it appeared as if he were going to pat me on the head, like an errant child. Then he seemed to think better of the idea.

He stood and walked over to the door. "I think ten thousand dollars for a day's work is a real effort. Fish's gone to look for a boat. Like I said, behave and I'll make sure Fish does the same. I don't know what you did to piss him off, but he's looking for an excuse to beat the shit out of you."

The pain took a back seat to the growing realization of what he had in mind for me. I closed my eyes for a moment, and then forced them open when consciousness began to slip away. "What's the boat for?" I asked.

"That was Fish's idea. After all, we need to get you out into the bayou. I don't want anyone seeing my boat going out into the bay." He gave a dismissive shrug of his shoulders, stepped out of the room, and pulled the door closed behind him.

They say that when a person looks death in the eye his life flashes before him. I didn't experience that. Instead, I struggled with my bonds until the ache in my skull became the major focus in my life, and then I passed out.

When I came to, Rusty was back in the room, searching through the closet. He must have heard me stirring because he looked my way.

"I thought maybe you were already dead." He dragged a jacket from the closet and threw it over his shoulders before continuing. "I don't know why I have Fish do anything. He steals a boat, and then gets the damn thing stuck in the river. Now I've got to go out and get him before it gets light and he gets caught."

My headache had eased, and I was glad to find that my mind was working again. I decided to play on Rusty's sympathies, if he had any. "It's not too late to let me go," I said.

"You're wrong there, Wes," he said, as he strode across the room and out the door.

A few moments later I heard the outer door slam shut. Swinging my feet over the side of the bed I stood, fighting to keep my balance.

The trip to the bedroom door seemed to take forever. I'd hop two steps, totter, and then fight to keep my legs beneath my body. Then I'd do it all over again. When I reached the door it was locked, but it seems Fish wasn't the only one who could screw things up. Like all bedroom doors, the latch was on the inside.

My hands, tied behind my back, were numb, so I fumbled for a good five minutes before I heard the latch click and I was able to get the door open. It gave with an outward lurch, and I hopped half a dozen stumbling steps before doing an ungracious dive to the floor where I smacked my head.

Fortunately, both the carpet and my head were thick, and within a short time I managed to get back to my feet and struggle into the kitchen. It took only a moment to find a knife and cut myself free.

It felt as if a thousand tiny teeth were gnawing at my hands and feet as the circulation returned to them. With the pain came feeling, and as soon as I could bear it I moved to the front door. Opening it a crack, I peered out into the night.

The breeze had freshened. Clouds hid the moon, and in the distance a bolt of lightning reached downward. The night air felt uninviting, and was heavy with the smell of brimstone.

My eyes opened wide and my heart raced when I saw Rusty's car still under the carport. I closed the door, ran to the rear of the house and peeked out a window. I was overcome with feelings of relief when I realized that Rusty's boat was gone.

I knew I should get as far away from Rusty's place as possible. Instead, I turned and began a sweep of the house in search of the manuscript.

I had no idea how long it would take Rusty to get Fish, or whether they would return by boat or Fish's truck. I did know I couldn't pass up this chance to look for the book.

My technique was as primitive as they come. Starting in the kitchen I began throwing open cupboards and pulling out pots and pans and dishes, letting them fall to the floor in a tumultuous drum roll.

Finding nothing, I worked my way through the living room and then the bedrooms. Again, I failed to find the manuscript, but while going through the closet of the bedroom where I'd been tied up, I came across a heavy, navy blue sweater that looked like it might fit me.

I tugged it over my sweatshirt, barely managing to stretch and pull the sweater on. It clung to me like a hungry boa constrictor and made me feel claustrophobic. I was tempted to pull it off, but it was a long walk home and cold outside. As an afterthought, I grabbed an unadorned baseball cap from the shelf and snapped it into place.

The one thing that stood out as I tore through the house was its state of disrepair. Windows were filthy. The kitchen was a total disaster. The faucet dripped. The floor was yellow and dingy. In the far corner a bucket, three quarters full of water, sat beneath a crack in the ceiling. All this indicated to me that Rusty had told the truth about being broke. Either that or he was a total slob. I suspected the truth was somewhere in between the two.

I spent another minute considering whether I had missed any possible hiding spots. A quick glance at my watch told me that too much time had passed and I needed to get the hell out of Rusty's house.

Halfway down the drive I tripped on a loose rock and fell to my knees. Mentally and physically exhausted, it dawned on me that a two minute drive amounted to a four or five mile hike. I hoped I was up to that kind of a trek in my present condition.

Making my way along Rabbit Creek Drive to Range Line Road, I cast an occasional look back over my shoulder. I was prepared to jump into the ditch or hide behind a tree at the first sign of either Fish or Rusty.

Once they discovered I was gone they would be out looking for me, and this made me leery of any approaching car. If they took Fish's truck back from the marina they could be in front of me, if they came back on Rusty's boat they could be coming up on my rear.

The service drive running from Rabbit Creek to Hamilton Boulevard was lined with small industrial businesses and, as a result, well lit. I knew it was the weakest link of my journey and so I was at my most alert. Every approaching set of car lights sent me scurrying for cover. I hid behind a truck trailer here, a small building there, until I reached the open field that separated the industrial park from Hamilton Boulevard. Here I hoped the dark would work to my advantage.

I had just moved into the field when a car turned off Hamilton onto the service drive. I looked around, and then bolted for a large tree just ahead of where I was walking.

Melding with the tree, I waited. A quick peek confirmed my worst fears as Fish's pickup sped past where I was hiding and turned onto Rabbit Creek Drive. It would be only a matter of minutes before they realized I had escaped.

Darkness was my refuge, but the first hint of gray was creeping into the eastern sky, so I started to jog across the field and by the time I saw a headlight moving my way, I was in the middle of the field with no place to hide.

The vehicle stopped and a beam of light spread out from the window as the car started back up and crept along the roadside. I ran a little farther, bent over, keeping as close to the ground as possible. Still, I realized I was moments away from being recaptured. That's when childhood games of hide and seek came to mind.

I had learned as a young boy that the best way to remain hidden was to stay out in plain view. If a person wore blue jeans and a dark sweater, like I was wearing tonight, it was possible to blend with the night by lying in the shadows. The other players would often walk right on by; their eyes sweeping past where they didn't expect to see anyone.

And so, as the car approached, I dove into a patch of long grass, stretched my body out as long and flat as I could, and hoped against all hope that they wouldn't spot me.

Burying my face into the grass I heard the car slow and sensed the beam of their spotlight flash by me. I forced myself to lie still for the count of a hundred and then I sprang to my feet and ran as fast as I could toward the tree line. The car stopped and swung around when they reached the end of the service drive, and once again I threw myself onto the ground and waited.

The ground was moist and smelled of moss and dead grass. I was running out of energy as we played hide and seek for three more passes, and then they pulled out onto Hamilton Road and headed off toward the marina, still creeping along, still shining the damn light. It was a good thing for me they had moved on, because the sky was graying and I was afraid I couldn't stay out of their sight for too much longer.

Mud covered and shivering, I trudged along Hamilton toward the Chevron station at the corner of D.I.P., where I hoped I could warm myself up and call Roy for a ride. Unfortunately, when I reached the station Rusty's car was parked out front. Skirting the store I continued my trek for the last mile and a half to the marina.

I almost lost the game when I turned onto Bayou Road. Glancing over my shoulder, I had just checked to make sure that Rusty's Caddy wasn't headed my way when I smelled a burning cigarette. Dropping to the ground, I rolled into the sewage ditch as Fish came walking up the street. If he had looked over his right shoulder he would have seen me, but he was talking on a cell phone as he stepped past my hiding space.

I was prepared to jump up and run if he turned, but he kept walking and talking. "He hasn't been here, Rusty."

There was silence, and then he said, "Yeah. Well, come get me and we'll head back to your place. I don't think he'll go to the police. He's just dumb enough to come back to the house. We can be ready for him. Besides, you're selling the book tomorrow, aren't you?"

Then he drifted out of my hearing range. I kept my head down and lay still in the ditch until I heard the tires of a car pull off the road. There were voices, and then a door slammed and the car pulled away. That's when I looked up and saw the taillights of Rusty's car heading back toward Hamilton.

By the time I reached the parking lot, all I could think about was taking a hot shower and climbing into bed. I dragged my weary body down the dock, looking forward with each step to calling it a day, only to discover an empty slip. My boat was gone.

Chapter 16

I ran to the end of the dock and gazed out along the river. *Rough Draft* was half a mile upstream, sitting there, waiting for the tide to come in and break her loose.

Curling up and going to sleep right there in the middle of the dock was a tempting option at the moment. Instead, I trudged back down the dock, across the parking lot and over to Cathy's boat. Along the way I noticed that Rusty's trawler was back in its slip.

I fought the urge to break in and search it for the manuscript, but daylight was creeping across the sky. People would soon be wandering around, and if I didn't recover my boat before the tide turned, I might lose it all together. I'd once seen a boat break loose from its anchor and drift ashore. The damage to the bottom had been pretty extensive.

I was surprised to find Cathy's lights on, and when I knocked, she threw open the door. The pleasant scents of hot coffee and bacon wafted from within and my mouth began to water.

"Jesus, Wes," she said. "What the hell have you been up to? You look like shit."

"It's been a rough night. Any chance I can get a cup of coffee and maybe a little bacon?"

She wrinkled her nose but stepped aside. "Come on in."

Randy Travis played on the stereo, and bacon sizzled in the kitchen giving the place a down home flavor. Her houseboat was roomy and inviting. From the outside it appeared tiny, inside it was a bastion of efficiency. The kitchen and dining area were on the entrance level. There was a refrigerator, a stove with oven, an apartment sized, stacking, washer and dryer, and plenty of cupboard space. A small wood table with four chairs sat in the middle of the dining area.

Two steps down was the living room. A floral patterned loveseat, a matching rocker, and a desk with her computer shared the room with a thirty-two inch flat screen TV. Beyond the living room I could see her bedroom.

She poured us both a cup of coffee, put on a couple more strips of bacon, and scrambled half a dozen eggs. I filled her in on my nighttime excursions in between sips of hot coffee and forkfuls of bacon and eggs.

As she listened, she stood, walked over to her desk, and dug around through the bottom drawer. She came back and placed an Alabama information calendar on the table next to my plate. Opening it to February she pointed to the date. "High tide's a little after noon today. Do you think your boat will float free or do you think you'll need a tow?"

I leaned back in the chair, rested my hands on my stomach, and fought to keep my eyes open. "I don't know. It gets shallow quick up there. I suspect Fish Conners never had to deal with the deep draft of a sailboat.

"I came over to see if you'd take me out to *Rough Draft* in your dinghy. Mine's gone. I can only hope it's still with the boat."

Cathy picked up our plates and carried them over to the sink. "I'm expecting Rob at any minute now. In fact, you just finished his breakfast."

"That would be the ex?"

Cathy turned from the sink. "Yeah."

I yawned. "I'll go see if Cajun Bob can haul me there."

"No. I can do it. But we might as well wait until the tide starts coming in. In the meantime, why don't you use my shower? It's off the bedroom. And then you need to take a nap."

"Won't that be awkward? Explaining to your ex-husband why another man is sleeping in your bed?"

"I don't give a rat's ass whether he likes it or not. Might do him some good. Why don't you go take a quick shower and lie down? While you're doing that, I'll throw your clothes in the washer."

It was all I could do to keep from falling asleep right where I sat so I pushed myself up from the table and tottered back to the bathroom. I stripped, set my mud-stained clothing outside the door, and took one of the fastest showers I've ever taken. I couldn't wait to climb into that bed.

***

147

It was a long journey from dreamland to reality, and I fought the entire way. I pushed away the insistent hands that rocked my body, tried to ignore the calling voice. When I rolled over, I was staring up into Cathy's face.

"What time is it?" I asked.

"Ten-thirty." There was a tinge of raw anger in Cathy's voice. "The tide is beginning to come in. If you don't get out to the boat pretty soon it might work itself loose. We both know what happens then—bye bye *Rough Draft*."

I looked around. "If you'll hand me my clothes, I'll get dressed."

She grabbed my clean clothes off the chair where she'd set them while I'd been asleep, and threw them at me. Without another word she turned and stomped out of the room.

I couldn't think of anything I'd said or done to get her pissed at me so when I stepped out of the bedroom I asked, "Did I do something wrong?"

"The son of a bitch called at the last minute and said he wouldn't be here until tomorrow. I told him to go to hell."

"We must be talking about…."

"That asshole, Rob. This is so like him. He is the most undependable, uncaring person I've ever known."

"And the reason you still love him is?"

Cathy was pacing back and forth across the little kitchen. She stopped in front of the sink, picked up a towel, threw it back down and turned to face me.

Hands on hips, she gave me the look that all men should recognize as meaning, *Caution, don't go there*. "I don't still love the son of a bitch. At least I don't think I do." She lowered her voice as she added, "And don't you start on me, Darling. I don't need your shit on top of his."

The caustic use of my last name told me it was time to change the subject. "Maybe we should go check on my boat."

"My dinghy's gassed and ready to go." She threw me that look again before stalking off across the room and out the door.

Cajun Bob, Phil, Renee, and two of the other Bobs were standing at the end of the dock, looking out at *Rough Draft*, talking and pointing. The buzz stopped when they saw us.

"Tough luck, Wes." Cajun Bob nodded toward my boat. "If you need some help let me know. I'll come out in my boat and try to pull you loose." He held up a handheld VHF radio and added. "I'm tuned to channel sixty-eight."

I waved my thanks to the dockside supervisors. "I wonder what they think happened." I said as Cathy turned up the engine and headed upriver.

"I saw Renee this morning and told her someone set your boat adrift last night. She wanted to call the police but I told her not to bother. I figured you needed sleep more than you needed the marine police out here grilling you."

"Thanks," I said, as Cathy brought the dinghy up next to my boat.

"Any time," she snapped, and I wondered if I was on her permanent shit list.

I grabbed the ladder and pulled the inflatable forward until they touched. As I scrambled from the dinghy the inertia kicked the small boat away. Clutching at the rail I climbed aboard and into the cockpit.

Below, Fish had left a mess, although as I looked around I couldn't see any obvious physical damage to the boat itself.

I switched on the engine blower. While I waited for the blower to clear any fumes from the engine room, I walked the deck. Nothing appeared damaged so I headed back to the cockpit.

The key was in the ignition and the engine started with the first try. My unease gave way to relief and I waved Cathy away from the side of the boat.

This area of the river ran just a shade over six feet in depth at high tide, which meant that Fish had buried the keel five or six inches in the mud. The river bottom was soft and I wasn't too worried about any damage being done to the boat below the waterline. Still, I didn't know exactly how far off the channel Fish had driven the boat before running it aground.

I put her into gear, nothing. I shifted her into reverse, again nothing. Then I threw her into forward, turned the wheel hard, and felt the first shifting.

I moved the gearshift back and forth several times, and with each maneuver I swung the wheel, first to port and then to starboard, and like a stumbling elephant, the boat began to turn away from the bank of the river.

It was my intention to swing the boat around and hope that I could follow the track in the mud where Fish had first driven her aground. By turning the boat around I also broke the suction hold the mud had on my keel.

It was a nerve-racking exercise, but the boat eased forward until it gave a final lurch and pulled away from its resting place.

Cathy and Cajun Bob were waiting for me when I pulled up. With their help I got the boat tied up and the electrical supply reconnected.

"Thanks," I called out as Bob wandered away.

Cathy waited to say anything until we were alone. "Sorry I snapped at you. Sometimes Rob pisses me off so badly I can't stand any man."

"Why don't you come on inside and I'll put on a pot of coffee," I said.

She hesitated, then nodded and stepped aboard. "They did a real job on your stuff," she said, as she followed me below.

Most of my cupboards and shelves had been emptied, the contents dumped on the floor. I dug around until I found my grinder, and an unopened bag of coffee, then I got a pot started. Settling down on the starboard cushion, which for some reason was free of debris, I looked over at Cathy and said, "I don't know what he had in mind unless he was looking for cash. If he was, he didn't find any. That's what I love about cash cards."

The coffee was sputtering to an end and she waved me back down as I stood. "I'll get it," she said.

I plopped back down, watched for a minute while she picked two unbroken mugs off the floor, and then I drifted off to sleep.

It was an innocent sleep filled with pleasant dreams and uninterrupted. I awoke with a start. Daylight was fading, the boat rocked in the wind, and Cathy was gone.

Somehow, she had managed to straighten the mess around me. The place smelled of pine cleaner and bleach and everything was off the floor. My clothes were folded and stacked on the settee across from me and she'd even filled the shelves over the bunk where I'd fallen asleep.

I felt refreshed for the first time in days. I felt like I could go all night again. I was dying to get aboard Rusty's boat, but it was too early. Instead, I changed my clothes, tucked my wallet into my back pocket, and walked over to Cathy's boat.

I couldn't remember if she was working that night, but she answered my knock with a warm smile. "Come on in," she invited.

"Actually, I was thinking that I owe you a dinner, for your help this morning."

"You don't owe me a thing," she said. "In fact, I owe you for the way I treated you earlier."

"Let me rephrase my statement. I'm starving, and I really don't want to eat alone."

"In that case, let me grab a sweater and turn off the TV."

A few moments later she joined me, carrying a light blue sweater and a small purse. We strolled, arm-in-arm along the dock and across the parking lot. Occasionally the vague scent of her perfume tickled my senses.

The night was clear and brisk and as we approached the marina restaurant the aroma of roasting meats and fried fish set my mouth to watering.

I hadn't eaten since breakfast and family troubles, illuminated manuscripts, even near death experiences were the farthest thing from my mind.

While we ate our steaks, I tried to put aside any thoughts of the manuscript, Rusty, and Jessica. Everything came rushing back, however, when Cathy asked, "Did you call your cousin?"

"I lost my cell phone last night," I said.

"I left my phone on the boat," Cathy said. "When we're done eating if you want to walk me back I'll be glad to let you use it. I like her by the way, Jessica that is."

I thought I detected a touch of resentfulness in her voice and I wondered if she wasn't jealous.

I pushed aside my plate and changed the subject. "What's the latest with the ex?"

"The asshole called to say he had some business to take care of before he came down. Based on past experience, I took that to mean that he met a woman and couldn't leave until he slept with her."

"Are you going to get mad at me again if I repeat my earlier question?" I asked.

"What question would that be?"

"Are you still in love with this man?"

Avoiding my gaze, Cathy used her fork to move a piece of steak around her plate. "I don't know that I love him half as much as I need him to stop his philandering and love me. It's almost as if I need to prove to myself that our breakup hurt him as much as it hurt me. Pretty macabre, huh?"

The waitress came by and we both ordered coffee and key lime pie. When we were alone again, I asked, "And what does all this have to do with what you call the bad boy syndrome?"

Cathy looked up from her plate. "You're not really listening to what I'm saying, are you?"

"It's that obvious?"

She nodded.

"Sorry," I said. "But I can't get my mind off that damn manuscript. I keep wondering if Rusty hid it on his boat."

"You're not going to do something stupid?" she asked. "Are you?"

"I'm going to get onto *Carpe Diem*, and see if I can find the damn thing."

Cathy shook her head and began to chew on her lower lip. "If you get caught, they'll kill you."

"How long can it take to go through the boat?" I asked. "Ten minutes? Once the restaurant and the store close it gets pretty deserted around here."

"At least call your cousin, or better yet your uncle."

I shook my head. "I need to get aboard as soon as I can. If Rusty shows up he'll probably move the boat. It's now or never. Maybe you could call Roy for me. Let him know what I'm up to."

Cathy peered over her coffee cup. "Did you call him when you got up and let him know what happened?"

"I couldn't. Like I told you, Rusty took my cell phone."

"You could have used the store phone," Cathy pointed out.

"Well I didn't."

Cathy sighed. "Sometimes you're a stubborn buffoon. You should wait for help. You're going to get yourself killed, Wes. It sounds like Rusty's playing for keeps."

"Does that mean you won't call?"

"You're going to do this no matter what I do, aren't you?"

I forced a laugh, trying to sound less nervous about my plans than I really felt. "I don't have a choice."

"Bullshit. I'll call, but don't expect me to show up at your funeral. Give me the damn number."

"You have a pen or a pencil?"

She drew a pen from her purse, placed it on top of a clean napkin, and pushed it across the table. I wrote the number on the napkin and handed it to her. After she read it back to me she stood and walked out of the restaurant without another word.

I motioned for the waitress to bring our bill, and then picked at my pie while she took my card and brought back the receipt. I gulped down the remainder of my coffee and headed out into the night, following the dock to Rusty's boat.

Chapter 17

I stopped back at my boat for a flashlight, and then scouted the area around Rusty's boat to make sure no one was watching. When I was certain I was alone, I stepped aboard Rusty's boat, *Carpe Diem*.

There are hundreds, if not thousands, of boats throughout the United States with that name. 'Seize the day' was an appropriate thought if not an original one.

The boat was beautiful, expensive, and locked. A quick search of the deck turned up a boat hook and I used it to pry open the sliding doors. Boats are not made to keep people out and it was a simple task to spring the latch without doing any damage to the door or the lock itself. Once I was inside, I relocked the latch and began my search.

Switching on my flashlight, I moved throughout the boat, pulling curtains and drapes closed before proceeding. The boat was a masterpiece of craftsmanship. Rich, well-varnished teak had been used in abundance for the walls and cupboard doors. Some of it was carved, although the uncut areas were beautiful in their simplicity.

A large circular window dominated the wall that separated the galley from the main salon. Shining my light on the window brought out the lines of a dolphin etched into the pane, giving it an eerie glow.

I started with a cursory search of the galley. I checked drawers, cupboards, even the refrigerator, no manuscript. Then I took my search into the main salon.

Again, there was an abundance of beautiful teak. The thick, creamy carpet was sculptured, and spotless. The ivory leather settee cushions were smooth and tanned. Not the most practical choices for a boat. Keeping everything clean in a boating environment would have been my biggest concern.

The boat had two staterooms. The largest came equipped with a queen-size bed, two dressers and a large bathroom with a three-quarter-size bathtub.

I found the manuscript in the third drawer of the starboard dresser, tucked under a pair of jeans. It was wrapped inside two large Zip-lock bags. Stifling the urge to inspect the book, I grabbed it and ran back through the boat.

As I reached the galley the boat rocked. The door rattled and metal doorframe on metal sliders alerted me that someone was on board. Scurrying back into the bedroom, I returned the book to its hiding place under the jeans, and slid the drawer closed before slipping into the bathroom. Just in time. A rising cacophony of voices trailed through the boat and then Rusty stepped into the stateroom.

"I can't believe you left the book here," Rusty said.

"I thought it would be safer, what with Wes being at your house."

I could hear the drawer opening in the other room and I froze in place, afraid that any movement on my part would give my presence away.

The drawer closed and Rusty said, "You're lucky it's still here. Wes could have found it so easily."

"He ain't got the cajones to break in here after what we've put him through," Fish said.

"Don't kid yourself. He's been right on our tail since he started looking for the manuscript. Somehow he's managed to get out of our sights twice when we had him prisoner. He may have the biggest balls you've ever seen, Fish."

"Bullshit. If I see the bastard again, I'll shoot him. I've still got his gun."

"Just so he doesn't take it away from you," Rusty said. "Why don't you drive your truck back to the house, I'll bring the boat along. And leave that gun here in case Wes has a little more backbone than you give him credit for."

The boat shifted and then gave a little bounce as Fish climbed off. Voices buzzed, but I couldn't make out what was being said. When the engine started the boat vibrated beneath my feet. I had found the manuscript, but was on the verge of losing it. If I was lucky, I could grab the book and slip from the boat while Rusty was busy.

I crept from the bathroom to the stateroom, opened the drawer, and felt around inside. Nothing. Rusty must have taken the manuscript with him, or given it to Fish to take back to the house.

As I moved through the boat I listened to the sounds above me as Rusty walked about the pilothouse. Along the way I searched for the book. When I reached the galley I heard Rusty start down the steps. Dropping to my knees, I crawled under the table and drew back into the shadows.

The door slid open with a metallic groan. The acrid stench of cigar smoke filled the room. The galley floor creaked and bottles rattled. This was followed by the tinkle of a bottle cap tossed onto the counter. Then Rusty stepped back outside. He walked along the deck and I heard him whip the dock lines from the pilings. A moment later we were floating free.

Rusty hurried back up the ladder to the controls, put the motor in gear, and backed out of his slip. It was time for me to get the hell off this boat.

The odds were stacked against my retrieving the manuscript at this time, so I rolled out from beneath the table, scrambled over to the door and out into the cockpit just as we rounded the no wake sign. I looked up at the pilothouse and could see that Rusty was busy watching where he was going. I steeled my nerves, took three steps, and vaulted over the rail as Rusty poured on the gas.

The water shocked my system, driving away my breath and leaving me stunned. It felt thick and resisted my efforts to pull myself upward. When I broke through to the surface I treaded water for a moment, took my bearings, and set off toward the dock and my boat, which was a hundred yards away.

My swimming style was a modified breaststroke. For every foot my arms drew me forward, my shoes and clothing tried to drag me back. I breathed a prayer of thanks as the current and outgoing tide pushed me along, and in a few minutes I slammed up against one of the pilings. I grabbed on and held tight, fighting to regain my breath, hoping I had enough strength left to pull myself from the river.

Help arrived in the guise of Roy. "Wes." He called out from above. "I'm going to throw you a rope. Tie it around yourself and we'll help you out of the water." I didn't know where he had come from, and I didn't give a damn. I was shivering so hard I didn't think I'd be able to get out of the water by myself.

The rope splashed off to my left and I called up to him, "Back a little." Roy retrieved the rope and this time when he tossed it, it slapped against me.

As I grabbed for it I lost my hold on the piling. With the end of the rope clutched in my right hand, I let myself drift to the next pole, wrapping my legs around the post. I used a bowline knot to tie the line around my waist. Reaching up, I grabbed onto the dock and let my legs float free.

Two sets of hands grabbed my arms and the rope tightened around my waist, dragging me up and out of the river. Lying back, fighting for breath, I looked up into the worried eyes of Jessica, Cathy and Roy.

"You dumb shit." Jessica dug her toe into my side. "What the hell were you thinking, jumping off a moving boat like that?"

"It seemed like a good idea at the time," I said.

"You could have been hurt," Cathy said.

"I'm a good swimmer. Rusty has Roy's Colt, and I'm not in the mood to face any more guns. I did get my hands on the manuscript though."

"Where is it?" Jessica pushed her foot into my ribs again.

"That hurts," I said. She didn't seem to hear me.

"You didn't take it into the water with you, did you?"

"You think I'm stupid?"

"After that stunt, yeah," Jessica said.

Ignoring her I sat up and began working on the knotted rope around my waist. The bowline is designed to secure a heavy load, but can be untied under the most severe of conditions, including when wet. Despite my numb fingers, I picked it loose and tossed the line onto the dock.

Roy moved alongside of me and reached his hand down. I took hold and he levered me to my feet. "It's on the boat then?"

"I had my hands on it, but Fish and Rusty showed up before I could get away with it."

"Did he know you were on board?"

"No. I hope he didn't see me get off either. It's why I jumped like that. I didn't want Rusty to know that I found the book."

"I don't think he saw you, he was up in the pilothouse watching where he was going," Cathy said. "The only reason we did, is because we were watching for you. When Jessica and Roy showed up I told them you had gone to check out Rusty's boat."

"I've got to change," I said through chattering teeth. "I'm damn tired of being cold."

"Go ahead," Roy said. He picked up the line and handed it to me. "I took this off your boat. We'll meet you down in the parking lot. I think it's time for an all out assault on Rusty's house. I'm tired of this shit."

It took five minutes to change my clothes, and I had to settle for a paint-stained pair of sneakers I kept around for working on the boat.

When I came out of the boat I found Cathy seated on the dock, feet hanging over the side, staring into the dark depths. Roy and Jessica were nowhere to be found and I assumed they were waiting for me in the parking lot.

I figured they could wait a minute and sat down next to her. "Something wrong?" I asked.

She swung her feet for several moments and then looked over at me. There were tears in her eyes and her voice caught when she spoke. "When I saw Fish and Rusty climb on board that boat I thought you were a dead man."

"You were watching?"

She nodded. "I was worried. It scared the shit out of me when you went flying off the boat."

"Worried for a friend?" I asked.

"I don't know. Maybe. I'm confused about my feelings."

"And Rob?"

"More confusion."

"What are you saying?"

"I've been telling myself I'm still in love with Rob. I thought you were Mr. Nice Guy. Now I've seen a little of your rough side and I guess I'm more attracted than I want to admit."

I put my arm around her and when she looked up I kissed her. It was a tentative kiss but when she didn't pull away I kissed her again.

Cathy returned the kiss and with unexpected strength she pushed me down onto the dock and reached for my belt buckle. I tugged her shirt out of her pants and ran my fingertips over her breasts. Our kisses became more heated, and then Jessica's voice called out from the darkness.

"Maybe the two of you should get a room, or at least go back to one of your boats," she said.

"Shit." I pulled away from Cathy and fumbled with my belt. "What the hell are you doing sneaking up on us like that?" I asked.

"I wasn't sneaking up." The dock vibrated as Jessica walked over and stood above us. "And I don't want to interfere in your love life, but Roy sent me to find out what was taking you so long."

I jumped up, held out my hand and helped Cathy to her feet. "I guess I got distracted," I said.

"I've got to get going," Cathy said. "Call me in the morning, Wes." She gave my hand a squeeze and skipped past Jessica, leading the way down the dock. When we got to the parking lot she shot me a quick glance over her shoulder and ran off toward her boat.

Roy was closing the trunk to Jessica's car when we got there. He held out a set of keys. "I'm going to leave my truck here for you to drive," he said.

As I put the keys in my pocket he unclipped a cell phone from his belt. "Jessica told me you lost yours. I've used this thing maybe six times since I got it. Use it until you can replace yours. Jessica's number and my home number are in the contact list."

"Thanks." I said. "We'd better get going if we want to catch Rusty."

We drove in silence and as we turned onto Hamilton I said, "Turn onto the service drive for Range Line Road."

When we came up to Rabbit Creek Road, Roy pulled over at my direction and cut the engine. "He's just down the road," I said. "If we get any closer he might see us."

Roy jumped out of the car and ran to the trunk. He reached in and came back out holding two hunting rifles. He handed one to Jessica and one to me, and then he pulled out the assault rifle.

"No games this time," he said.

"What's the plan?" Jessica asked.

"We hit 'em before they know we're here," Roy said. "Jessica and I'll go in the front door. Wes, you hit the back. How's that sound?"

"It can't end up any worse than the last time," I said. I was tired of pussy footing around. It was time to put an end to all this nonsense and get the damn manuscript back. I checked to make sure the safety was off on my gun, and struck out toward the house followed by Roy and Jessica.

Chapter 18

A s we started up Rusty's driveway Roy took the lead, followed by Jessica, with me in the rear. The order had not been pre-arranged, but was rather the pecking order established by our previous outing.

Roy stopped and we crowded around him. "I don't see Fish's truck," he said. "You've been here before, Wes. Is there any place where it could be parked that we can't see?"

"I don't think so." I pointed up the hill toward the house. "He was parked behind Rusty's Cadillac before. He must not be here."

"That makes it easier," Roy said. "Lights are on so I say we go in and get the damn book. Wes, why don't you go around back, Jessica and I will hit him from the front. If we're lucky the doors will be open, but I'm crashing in if they're not. You ready?"

Bent low, I took off running at an angle across the yard toward the back of the house, not stopping until I reached the back wall. When I poked my head around the corner I noticed the boat was gone. No truck. No boat. Maybe no one was at home.

Pressing my body against the siding of the house, I slid over to the door, reached out, and found it locked. A moment later I heard a crash from the front of the house as Roy broke through the door. I stepped back, let out a kick, and threw my shoulder against the cracked doorframe.

Holding my gun pointed in front of me I ran through the kitchen and out into the living room.

Jessica spun around as I burst into the room and lowered her gun when she saw me. "Uncle Roy's checking out the bedrooms," she said. Her eyes were wide, her face flushed with excitement.

"I don't think he'll find anything," I said. "The boat's gone."

Roy walked into the room in time to hear me. "Wes, I know you saw the manuscript on Rusty's boat. But we should still do a quick search of the house. I suspect Rusty keeps it with him, but we'd be nuts not to look. Why don't you take the kitchen? Jessica, you stand guard and I'll check out the bedrooms. We'd better be quick about it though. The last thing we need is for the police to show up."

I scoured the kitchen, but once again found nothing. I headed for the living room where I found Jessica leaning against the wall, peeking out from behind the curtains.

"All clear so far," she said.

"I'll go check on Roy," I said. As I turned toward the bedroom I caught sight of a cell phone sitting on the arm of the sofa.

"I'll be damned," I said. Plucking the phone from its resting place I flipped open the cover and shook my head.

"What?" Jessica dropped the corner of the curtain and moved over to join me.

"It's mine."

Roy walked into the room. "We'd better get going."

Tucking the phone into my pocket I unclipped Roy's from my belt and held it out for him. "I don't need two of the damn things. One gets me into enough trouble."

Roy grabbed the phone as he crossed to the front door. He cracked it open, looked around, and stepped out into the night. "Let's get the hell out of here."

As we drove back to the marina my thoughts turned from the manuscript to my new family. Jessica and Roy were no longer strangers from a strange land, although I had to admit Alabama had its share of strange.

When we arrived at the marina, Jessica parked the car and turned to face me. "If you go chasing around by yourself again, I'll kill you myself. That is if Fish and Rusty don't beat me to it."

"I think she means it, son." Roy slid out of the back seat and stood by the passenger door, waiting for me to get out. When I did, he put his left hand on my shoulder and drew a nine-millimeter pistol from his coat pocket. "You'd better take this." Then, in a fatherly fashion he added, "Try not to lose this one. And you should listen to Jessica. The book isn't worth your life, or any of our lives for that matter. Understand?"

I slipped the gun into my waistband. "If I hear, see or feel anything, I'll call."

"We're here for you Wes," he said. "Just remember that."

Something in the tone of his voice drew my attention to his weathered face. His eyes were filled with genuine concern and without thinking, I said, "Would the two of you like to come down to the boat and have a drink before you head out?"

Jessica switched off the engine and was out of the car almost before I finished asking. "Let's go," she said. As she swung around me she grabbed Roy's arm and headed toward the dock.

I watched the two of them for a moment, and then I hurried along, trailing them out to my boat. I was dead tired again and couldn't for the life of me understand what had possessed me to extend this invitation.

The night air had a salty feel to it. In the distance the engines of a large ship echoed across the still bay, bound for ports unknown. I was beginning to get itchy feet, and I wished I was tagging along beside that behemoth, riding the waves instead of chasing an old book around Mobile, Alabama. I longed to once again be carefree and headed for nowhere.

We paraded onto *Rough Draft* and down into the cabin. I made a waving motion toward the empty berths as I stopped at the galley and opened the cupboard where I kept my extra mugs. "Sit anywhere. I've got Miller Lite or rum and Coke. And if you'd prefer, I think I can rustle up some pineapple juice to go with the rum."

"Rum over a little ice for me," Roy said.

I pulled the gun from my pants and laid it on the counter. "I don't have any glasses," I said. "Just plastic mugs. Glass and ceramics don't hold up well in a storm."

It took me a moment to gather three mugs together. One of the drawbacks of living on a boat is limited space. Livaboards, as those of us who live on a boat are called, tend to bury unused items beneath seats or in corners, often under items used every day. Since I live alone, I only keep two mugs handy on the oft chance another boater might drop by. Finding a third was a chore.

I tossed three ice cubes into a mug, topped it with a hefty splash of rum, and handed it to Roy. They were both seated on the starboard sofa.

Jessica looked uncomfortable with her arms folded across her chest. The pained frown she wore was unpleasant and added years to her face. Roy seemed relaxed and was either unaware of the volcano seated beside him waiting to erupt, or so used to Jessica's moods that he didn't care. On the other hand, I was getting damned tired of her attitude.

I had no idea what I'd done to piss her off this time, but I decided to play it cool. "How about you?" I asked her.

"Just a Coke." Her voice turned frosty as she added, "Diet if you have it."

"Certainly your highness." I reached into the fridge, pushed aside a diet Coke and pulled out my last regular Coke. I can be as passive-aggressive as the next person. I gave the can a little toss. She fumbled it, dropping the unopened Coke into her lap. The glare she shot me was enough to freeze a steam pipe. She popped the top without a word and I handed her a mug before grabbing a Miller Lite for myself. Finally, I crossed over to the port settee and settled in.

169

Roy downed his drink in two long swallows, then smacked his lips. "Nothing like a little rum to help a man relax."

He waved me down when I started to reach for the empty cup and added, "I never have more than one. It's one of those habits I could find addicting, so I control the urge."

Roy set the mug on the counter and took a small, darkened pipe from his pocket, holding it up for my inspection. "My biggest vice, one I can't seem to control. Mind if I smoke?"

I have an unwavering rule on board; have had since the day I bought the boat. No smoking. Yet for some reason, I said, "Go ahead."

He took a pouch out of his other pocket and began to build his smoke. I couldn't help but smile at his little ritual. Scoop a little, tap the tobacco down, and scoop a little more. Almost as an afterthought, he pulled out an old Zippo lighter and lit the pipe.

The rich tobacco smoke spewed forth and filled the boat, wrapping us in a scented cocoon. There was a hint of anise or almond or perhaps cherry, I couldn't quite put my finger on it, but somehow it made me want to go out and buy a pipe.

Easing back into the cushions I sipped my beer and watched Jessica. She squeezed and released the can in her hand, playing a metallic symphony that was doing an excellent job of eroding my mellow mood. When I couldn't stand it any longer, I asked, "Something bothering you, Jess?"

Her head snapped in my direction and she gave me a cutting look. "I told you my name is Jessica."

Roy chuckled and pointed his pipe stem in my direction. "When she was six years old she beat the crap out of a neighbor boy for calling her Jess. Since that day I can't remember anyone calling her that and not suffering some consequence or another."

"You mean there's something worse than the silent treatment and that evil eye she keeps casting my way?"

"I'm not giving you the evil eye. If I were, you'd know it. It just so happens I was deep in thought. Something you don't seem too familiar with."

I raised my hands in mock defeat. "If there's something you want to say to me, why don't you just spit it out?"

"Fine." She drained the rest of her Coke. "Were you born an asshole, Wes?"

I was taken aback. "What do you mean?"

"Gran's going into the hospital next week and she's convinced she's not coming out. All she can talk about is how she wishes she could meet you and maybe talk to you a little."

"What's wrong with her?" I asked.

"You're being a little melodramatic," Roy cut in. "She's going in for a hip replacement and I don't remember her saying anything about being afraid she wouldn't make it through the surgery."

Jessica transferred her glare from me to Roy and he said, "I'll admit that she did say something about wanting to see Wes before she died. But I don't think she was talking about her imminent death."

"She told me too many people she knew were going into the hospital and not coming out," Jessica said. "If that's not expressing concern about dying, then what is?"

"You're right dear." Roy continued to look down at the pipe in his hand, studying it with exaggerated care, intent on backing away from the discussion.

"All right," I said.

Roy raised his eyes and looked at me without moving.

"All right what?" Jessica asked.

"All right, I'll go see her. Set up a time and place and I'll be there." My stomach did a little jig as I said the words, and my hands trembled. I had enough trouble interacting with my mother, let alone a grandmother who hadn't bothered to contact me in over thirty years.

Jessica jumped up, threw herself across the cabin and engulfed me with a hug. "You won't regret this, I promise."

I disengaged from her and said, "I'm not making any promises beyond the one visit. I still feel some resentment toward her."

Jessica grabbed Roy's hand and gave it a tug. "Come on, let's get out of here before he changes his mind." To me she added, "I'll talk to Gran tomorrow. Maybe we can do lunch?"

"I guess we can do that," I said, regretting my decision already.

"Good." Jessica raced up the stairs, towing Roy along behind her.

He paused on the top step and turned to me. "I've got a friend who owns a helicopter. I'll give him a call come daylight and see if he can fly us around. If Rusty's on his boat, we'll find him."

"If we don't find him soon the book's as good as gone," I said.

He gave a quick nod, and then followed Jessica out into the night.

Chapter 19

Alone, I took another beer from the fridge and stepped out into the cool night air. Time was running out and I dreaded the thought of defeat at the hands of Rusty and Fish.

Dispirited, with depression creeping up on me, I sat down in the cockpit, put my feet up, and sipped my beer. As I contemplated life's unfairness, I heard the sound of a boat motor in the distance. A few minutes later I saw the red port navigation light and the aft white light. Even though it was dark, I scooted down in the cockpit.

I was pretty sure it was Rusty's trawler, and as it motored by I managed to make out the name *Carpe Diem* on the transom. Rusty was headed home.

I slipped into the cabin and grabbed my phone to call Roy. He didn't answer. I picked up Roy's gun and stuffed it into the pocket of my sweatshirt where it dragged against the stretchy fabric. I'd promised not to go off half-cocked by myself, but I told myself it wasn't my fault Roy hadn't answered his phone. I clipped the phone to my belt, grabbed the truck keys, and hastened off the boat.

I tried Roy again as I pulled out of the parking lot. I considered calling Jessica, but I really didn't want her involved anymore. Instead, I pressed down on the accelerator and pointed the truck toward Rusty's place.

The house was lit up and Rusty's Cadillac was parked under the carport. To my relief, Fish's truck was nowhere to be seen. I parked one house down from Rusty's, and made the trek up the drive with my hand on the gun in my pocket, jumping at every night sound I encountered.

A quick check around the house confirmed that *Carpe Diem* was tied to the dock and that no one was lying in wait for me outside. At the front door I took a deep breath, pulled the automatic from my pocket and turned the knob.

Pushing open the door I was surprised to see Rusty seated in the lounge chair reading a book. On the table next to him was a large glass of brown tinted liquid and a cell phone. As I drew the door shut behind me he looked up, closed the book, and smiled. "I've been expecting you ever since I saw you slinking around in the cockpit of your boat."

"You don't seem concerned by the fact that I'm standing here pointing a gun at you." I looked around. "Why's that, Rusty?"

"That's because I've taken out an insurance policy." Placing his book on the table next to the phone, he picked up his glass. "Can I offer you a glass of sweet tea?"

I glanced across the room to the hallway leading off to the kitchen and bedrooms.

"You have nothing to worry about," he said. "We're alone. I've decided to try another approach, rather than kill you that is."

175

"And that would be?"

"Maybe you could put the gun down and we can talk about it."

"I don't think so." I moved two steps closer to Rusty so that I was standing over him. "Why don't you give me the manuscript and I'll leave you alone."

Rusty set his glass down and picked up the cell phone from the table. "There's someone you need to talk to," he said.

"Who?"

Rusty raised the phone and made a show of pushing a button, and then he held the phone out to me.

I snatched it from his hand and held it to my ear. "Who the hell is this?"

"Wes?" Cathy's voice trembled out from the phone. "Fish says he'll kill me if you don't listen to Rusty."

What she said was almost drowned out on her end by the piercing bray of a train horn.

"Where are you?"

"I don't know. I don't like the way he looks at me, Wes."

Before I could respond Fish's voice came on. "I owe you big time and it won't bother me to take it out on her. Then it's your cousin's turn. That bitch almost took my finger off. Now put Rusty back on the phone."

Rusty kept his side of the conversation brief. "Ah huh. Yup. Just stick to the plan. I'll take care of him."

"She has nothing to do with this," I said when Rusty put down the phone.

"And nothing will happen to her as long as you behave," he said. "Now you go on back to your boat, don't call your uncle, don't call Jessica. Sit tight and by noon tomorrow the book will be in the hands of its new owner. At that point I'll call and let you know where you can find Cathy. That way no one gets hurt, I get my money, and it's all over."

"If you hurt her, I'll kill you."

"An unnecessary threat," he said. "Now if you'll just close the door behind you when you leave."

"How do I know Fish won't hurt her?"

"He's on his way back here as we speak. Cathy will be left tied up in a place Fish assures me is safe and comfortable. I can control Fish as long as you behave. I'm hoping we can put this foolishness behind us. Good night, Wes."

I stared down at him for several moments, then turned and left. What else could I do? As soon as I got out to the truck I set the gun on the seat next to me and tried to call Roy again, but my phone was dead.

By the time I got back to the marina I thought I'd figured out where they were keeping Cathy. I remembered hearing the train when we were at Fish's place. It would be just like Fish to take Cathy back to his place, and when I thought about what he had tried to do to Jessica a cold finger of fear crept up my spine.

I was going to check out my theory with or without Roy's help, but I knew I had to let him know what I was doing. I didn't trust Rusty to live up to his side of the

177

bargain and I knew that if something happened to me, Cathy would be at Fish's mercy.

I parked the truck and ran to my boat. I knew my twelve volt phone charger was packed in a plastic box stored under the front berth. The problem was a dozen plastic boxes were piled under the berth.

Naturally, the charger was in the bottom box. I fumbled around until I found it, then I grabbed a flashlight and headed back out to the truck. As I drove out of the lot I plugged in the phone and tried Roy again. There was still no answer so I left a message telling him about Cathy and my theory that Fish had her at his place. I also asked him to meet me there if he got the message.

By the time I reached the turnoff to Fish's trailer, I'd managed to calm myself down. I was still worried about Cathy, but the truth of the matter was, my keeping a cool head about the whole thing was the only chance she had.

I parked the truck, climbed out, and took three deep calming breaths. Then I released the automatic's safety and started off into the woods at a brisk pace. The air was crisp and biting and smelled of apple wood and pine. Above, the night was clear and star filled.

I paused at the end of the wood line and looked around. The trailer was dark and appeared deserted.

Fish seemed like the kind of guy who was over confident and I suspected he might very well be sleeping. Then again it may be a trap. It didn't matter. I couldn't leave without checking the place out and seeing if Cathy was there.

I drew another deep breath and took off running along the tree line toward the back of the trailer. This time, without the rain and mud, the going was much easier. When I reached the front of the trailer I climbed the steps and stood listening for a good five minutes before reaching for the door latch.

The door was unlocked and it squeaked as I pushed it open. Again I stood and listened. I could hear the drip, drip, drip of a leaky water faucet off to my right. I took the flashlight from my pocket, switched it on, and started forward. The floor groaned, and I felt a knot begin to form between my shoulder blades. It began to itch like a giant mosquito bite, but I had the gun in one hand and the flashlight in the other so I couldn't scratch it.

I headed toward the bedroom, well aware that if Fish was there the floorboards were telling him he wasn't alone. Realizing I would not be able to sneak up on Fish, I crossed the room quickly.

The place was empty. No Fish. No Cathy. But someone had been there since I'd last visited. The bloody sheets had been removed from the bed and lay in a crumpled heap in a corner of the bedroom.

I moved back to the kitchen and there, lying next to a McDonald's takeout bag was a small brown wallet. I walked over, picked it up, and opened it. All that was inside was Cathy's driver's license.

Chapter 20

I turned and ran for the barn, the pistol held out in front of me. This time there was no light on in the building. When I reached the door I took out my flashlight and stood listening for about a minute. In the distance I heard the rumble of a train and somewhere off toward the highway a car engine sputtered to life.

The barn itself creaked and groaned as old buildings often do, but there were no voices. No sounds that indicated anyone was nearby. I slipped inside, crouched, and staying as deep in the shadows as possible extended the pistol in front of me.

I then held the flashlight in my left hand out to the side, as far away from my body as possible. I knew that if someone was waiting for me they were likely to shoot as soon as the light went on. I hoped if that happened they would shoot toward the light, which was now three feet from my body.

I turned on the flashlight. Nothing. No shots. No sounds of someone rushing toward me. No Fish. Just the old car sitting in the middle of the barn.

When I stepped outside I found Roy, rifle in hand, leaning against the side of the barn. He stood staring out into the night, watching and listening.

"I see you got my message," I said as I joined him. I tucked the pistol into my belt and asked, "You alone?"

Roy shook his head. "We got here just as you started running to the barn. I'd have followed you in but I was afraid you'd shoot me, so I decided to stand guard out here. I left Jessica at the trailer. I take it you didn't find Cathy."

"I found her wallet in the trailer, but she's not here." I said. "Looks like Rusty keeps the manuscript."

A branch snapped and Roy put a hand on my arm. He brought his rifle up, and I reached for my pistol, but it was Jessica who raced from the shadows. She was holding a phone book and seemed excited as she ran up to us.

"I think I know where Cathy is." She pushed the book into my hands. I took it from her, shined my flashlight on the open page, and looked at the heading: MOTELS.

"This doesn't tell us a thing." I said. There was a ring of disappointment in my voice and she snatched the book back from me, pointing to a small ad that had been circled in red.

Roy and I both leaned in and read:

Turner's Motel and rustic cabins.

Daily, weekly, monthly rates.

"What's the likelihood he took her there?" I asked. "He could have circled that ad months ago. And even if she is there, what do we do? Go up to the desk clerk and ask if Fish Conners came in with a kidnapped woman. I think we're just going to have to trust that they'll let her go once they sell the manuscript."

I started back toward the truck, but Jessica stopped me. "Don't be so pig headed, Wes. We can't trust Rusty, and we can't trust Fish. I'm telling you, the book was right next to the phone and the red pen was sitting on top of it. You've seen his place, what are the chances that he's organized enough to keep a specific pen with his phone book. If he used that pen, he did it today."

I moved away from Jessica, but Roy stepped in front of me. "She's right, Wes," he said. "It's worth a shot. An old classmate of mine, Leroy Parkens, owns the place. It's only a five minute drive. If she's not there, we let them have the damn book."

I stared at him for several moments, then looked over at Jessica and saw the excitement reflected in her eyes. "You're a regular Sherlock Holmes, after all," I said.

"I prefer Kinsey Millhone," she said. "Sherlock's a little too stuffy for me."

"Who the hell's Kinsey Millhone?" I asked.

"You mean you've never read any of Sue Grafton's books? You're not one of those guys who wouldn't think of reading a mystery by a woman, are you? What, a tough woman detective threatens your masculinity?"

Roy reached out, grabbed Jessica's arm, and began to steer her back toward the way we'd come. "This isn't a book club. This girl must be scared out of her wits and the sooner we find her the better. Besides, once we find her we can go after Rusty. I'm getting real sick of this guy."

Deep in thought, I followed them to the car. I no longer cared about getting the manuscript back. It wasn't right that Cathy had to suffer because my grandfather took a souvenir off of a dead German soldier over sixty years ago. If we didn't recover the book, so be it. But I'd be damned if I was going to let Rusty and Fish profit from its sale after this.

Jessica's car was parked in front of the truck and as we approached the vehicles Roy stopped and held out his hand. "Why don't you give me my keys. You can drive with Jessica and follow me."

Jessica didn't talk at all as we drove. I didn't know if she was mad at me or just concerned about Cathy. It was just as well, I was worried too and the quiet suited me.

The motel lot was dimly lit and in need of paving. Jessica slowed to a crawl and swerved to avoid a pothole while Roy plowed ahead to the closest parking space to the motel office. He was waiting at the door, tapping his left foot impatiently when we walked up.

"I didn't see Fish's truck," he said. "Did you?"

Jessica shook her head and I asked, "Is this the only place to park?"

"He could have driven it down by one of the cabins," Roy said. "Come on, let's go into the office and see what Leroy has to say."

The interior was paneled with smoke darkened knotty-pine planks. A leather couch and sofa, cracked with age, faced a small television set. A nineteen seventies era Mediterranean style hanging lamp cast a shadow along the walls, and an artificial palm tree stood next to the counter. A sign read: 'If you don't see me, try the buzzer'. In parenthesis, and capitalized, was the word 'ONCE'. An arrow pointed to a small button behind the palm tree.

Roy pressed the button. Somewhere, further back in the building, the buzzer reverberated like an ailing bullfrog. I looked at my watch and was surprised to see that it was almost three in the morning. No wonder it had been a battle keeping my eyes open on the trip over here.

After perhaps five minutes I reached over to press the button again but Roy caught my wrist. "Didn't you read the sign, boy?"

"I figured he must have gone back to sleep," I said. "Can't hurt to give it another try, can it?"

"You people come down here from up north and I swear ya'll are wound so tight I keep expecting you to start spinning around in circles as you walk. Leroy said once, he means once. Leroy's not a patient man. Ring that bell again and it just might piss him off. Then he's just as likely to tell us to get off his property and go to hell as help us."

"Not a very prudent way to run a service business," I said.

Roy shrugged. "Leroy doesn't need a lot to live on. He once told me that what he likes about working for himself is that nobody can make him work if he doesn't want to. Says he can invite the devil to dinner or tell him to go back to hell, and nobody sits around in an office and calls him on the carpet for doing it. He'll be out here shortly. That's a Southern shortly, not a Northern shortly."

As if he'd been waiting off stage for his cue, the door behind the counter opened and a small man in his mid-to-late fifties pushed into the room, bringing with him the fetid smell of stale tobacco and whiskey.

Dog River Blues

A fading tattoo of a naked woman ran the length of his lower left arm. He wore a pair of bib overalls that looked like they might have survived the Civil War, and although his arms and legs were pole bean skinny, he had one of the meanest beer guts I'd ever seen.

He nodded in our direction. "Roy. Whatever possessed you to think you could come out here and haul my ass out of bed at this time a night?"

"I'm looking for Fish Conners. Mick Conners' boy."

"I know Fish."

"He been here?" Roy asked.

Leroy scratched his belly. "Every once in awhile Fish comes by. Usually he wants a favor. Course I get a little scratch when I do him a favor."

Roy nudged my foot with his, held up his hand and rubbed his thumb across his fingertips. "Got any cash on you?"

I took out my wallet and drew a twenty from within. When I placed it on the counter Roy glared at me. He reached over and slid out another bill, which he placed on top of the first one.

Leroy picked up the bills, stuck them in his pocket, and said, "Ol' Fish, he come in here around ten this evening and told me he needed a cabin. Said he wanted to entertain a female friend and his place was a mess. I rented him number three out in the woods. Fish likes his privacy."

"You got a spare key to that cabin?" Roy asked.

Leroy licked his lips and tapped a finger on the counter where the two twenties had sat a moment earlier.

185

"That boy's got a mean streak and he don't even bother trying to hide it," he said. "I'm not sure I should help you."

"We're just playing a little joke on the man," Roy said. He nudged my foot again and nodded toward the counter.

I took out another twenty and when Roy prodded me again, I added one more to the pile. Spreading the wallet I said, "That's all I've got."

Roy's voice hardened. "You heard the man, Leroy."

Leroy licked his lips, and then grabbed the remaining bills. Crumpling them into his fist, he stuffed them into his pocket with the others. Then he shuffled back through the door and returned a moment later with a key on a plastic holder.

Tossing the key on the counter, Leroy said, "You been there before, Roy." He pointed to the door. "When you're finished, just leave the key in the box over there. I'm going on back to bed now. Try not to make too much noise out there, Roy." He gave us a sleepy nod, and then he walked out of the room, letting the door slam behind him as if to say he was through with us.

I pushed past Roy and Jessica, swung the door open, and went outside. A dense mantle of fog had settled over the area. It rose in thick tendrils from the ground, thinning only when it reached the uppermost branches of the surrounding trees. The air smelled as if it had been washed with pine scented soap. The parking lot was buried in a misty cocoon, and the cars moved in and out of focus like spectral derelicts in an ocean of opaque fleece. "Where to?" I asked, as Roy strode past me.

"Just follow me," he said, moving off into the thickening mist. Jessica joined me and before he could fade away I took her hand and hurried after him.

When we caught up to Roy, Jessica slipped her free hand through his arm, forming a chain.

"Can you find the cabin in this shit?" I asked.

"Quiet," Roy said. "I know where I'm going, but we don't want to give ourselves away if Fish is still here. There's no way we can spot his truck in this fog."

I shut up as we snaked our way across the parking lot and into the woods.

A low wattage light burned over the cabin door and inside a soft light cast a glow on the shaded window like Tinkerbell searching for the lost boys. Painted on the peeling door was the faded number *three*. Aware that Fish might be within, and unable to see whether his truck was parked nearby, we crept up to the door.

"I left my damn rifle in the car." Roy had lowered his voice to a whisper. "You got that nine millimeter with you?"

"I do."

He slapped me on the back. "Atta boy. So, either you go in first, or give me the gun."

I pulled the gun from my pocket, shouldered my way past him, and pointed at the lock. He reached over, inserted the key, and turned the knob.

I've done this plenty of times in the past. It never gets easier, and I'm always scared shitless. Taking a deep breath, I tried not to think about the consequences as I kicked open the door and dove into the room. I executed a quick shoulder roll and came to rest flat on my stomach, in the middle of the single room. Watching and listening, I lay there for the count of ten. A small nightlight, plugged in near the floor next to the bed, cast a weak beacon across the battered wood floor. I could make out the bulk features of the room. The bed, a small sofa, a table.

Something stirred on the mattress. I snapped up to one knee, pistol extended in front of me, and looked into Cathy's terrified eyes. I wanted to go to her. Instead, I got up into a crouch, gun in front of me, and edged across the room to the only other door. It stood ajar, and when I came closer, it revealed an empty bathroom.

"It's clear," I called out as I ran to the bed. Cathy's mouth was covered and she was bound hand and foot with duct tape. Gazing down at her I could read the relief in her eyes. Reaching out, I fingered the edge of the tape covering her lips. Someone snapped on the overhead light at the very moment that I stripped it from her lips, and I cringed at the look of pain that crossed her face as she screamed.

"I'm sorry," I said. "There's just no gentle way of doing that." Reaching out I touched her cheek, and as her sobs shook her body I sat on the bed and held her while she cried.

"He said he'd be back for me. I could tell he didn't mean it in a nice way."

As I comforted her, Roy went to work on the tape holding her. Cathy cried out several times when he pulled the tape loose, and once he had finished she tucked her face into my neck and wrapped her arms around me.

Along with the warmth of her tears against my cheek, I could feel her body tense.

I gently disengaged. "We've got to get out of here," I said. "There's no telling when Fish might come back."

She jumped from the bed as if I'd stung her with a cattle prod and stumbled across the room, tripping and almost falling with each step. Jessica crossed over to her. "It's cold out there," she said. Removing her coat she handed it to Cathy and added, "You're going to need this."

"What about you?" Cathy asked.

"I'll be fine," Jessica said. "I've got a sweater out in the car. Come on now, put it on."

As she took the jacket from Jessica, Cathy lowered her head. I walked over and touched her arm and she flinched.

"We'd better get going," Roy said. He led the way out of the cabin and back through the fog to the car.

Roy took his truck and Jessica drove the car back to the marina. I sat in the front seat and kept glancing back at Cathy. She made a pointed effort to ignore me. When we arrived back at the marina she began to whimper. "I can't go back there," she said. "That's where he found me. I was walking to my boat when he jumped out and grabbed me."

"You can come home with me," Jessica said.

Cathy considered the invitation for a moment, then nodded. "I'll need some things from the boat."

"I'll walk you down," I said.

"I can help," Jessica said. She stepped forward but Roy reached out and took hold of her elbow.

"We'll wait here for you," he said. "Jessica, why don't you wait in the car?"

"But...."

"Please," Cathy said. "I'd like a few minutes alone with Wes, if you don't mind."

"We'll be here," Roy said.

I took Cathy's arm and led her toward the dock. The closer we got to her boat the more drag she exerted on my hand until she stopped dead in front of her boat.

"He was waiting for me inside the door," she said. "I'd just run down to the marina store for a few things."

"You wait here," I said. "I'll check it out."

"No!" She gripped my hand hard enough to cause me pain and I looked down at her, waiting for her to tell me what she wanted me to do. "I don't want to be left alone," she said. "I'll come in with you."

I went in first, while Cathy stood at the door. When I gave the all clear she rushed past me to the bedroom. I sat down on the sofa and waited, listening to Cathy's activities at the other end of the houseboat. I wasn't too worried about Fish returning. I knew Roy would be watching from the parking lot.

Cathy dragged a suitcase and a backpack from the back of the boat and left them lying next to the sofa while she went to the galley and opened the refrigerator. "Can I get you something to drink?" she asked, as she pulled out a beer for herself.

"A Pepsi, if you have one."

"Just diet," she said. I nodded and she took out a can, popped the top and carried it and the beer over to the sofa and sat down next to me.

I leaned toward Cathy. "What now?"

190

"Know of anybody who might want to buy a houseboat?"

"You're kidding, right?" I studied her face and waited for a response.

She took a sip of her beer and looked away from me. "I don't think I'll ever feel safe here again. Even when this is all over, I'll be looking over my shoulder every time I walk out to the boat, waiting, never knowing who might be out there watching me."

"So what'll you do?"

"I don't know." She took a final slug of the beer, set the bottle on the floor, and eased up from the sofa. "For now, I'm going to take your cousin up on her invitation. We'll have to see what tomorrow brings. Come on, let's go."

I stood, set my Pepsi can on the table and reached around her for her bags. "I'm going to have a little talk with Fish Conners," I said. "When I'm done with him I don't think he'll bother anyone again."

She gave me a look I'd never seen in a woman before. "I hope you cut his balls off and make him eat them," she said. "Then kill the bastard."

She took a final look around the room and noticed her cell phone on the counter. She grabbed it and flipped it open. "Give me just a minute while I check this message."

She was close enough that I could hear a man's voice echo from the phone.

"Hey, cutie," he said. "I finally managed to get away. I'm looking forward to seeing you and holding you, it's been way too long. I've got my cell phone on and I'll be driving straight through, so if you get this message you can call me anytime during the night. I should be down there by noon tomorrow. Love ya."

I watched Cathy's shoulders slump as she listened. She closed the phone, tucked it into her back pocket, and wrapped her arms across her chest. Her body language seemed to say, "Damn," but when she looked up her eyes were lit, her lips pursed into a diminutive smile. I knew right then that she was going to take her ex back. As I led the way down the dock I wondered how long it would take her to realize she was making a mistake.

The fog had spread from the low-lying edges of the bay to wrap the marina in its nebulous grip. We would have walked right on by the car if Roy hadn't called, "Over here, Wes."

Cathy let out a little gasp at the sound of his voice and clutched at my hand.

"It's all right," I said. We changed direction and walked up to the car. I tossed Cathy's bags into the open trunk and slammed it closed. As Roy helped Cathy into the back seat, Jessica took her hand for support.

Roy and I drifted toward the driver's door and he handed me the truck keys. "We'll all go in the car."

"The fog's getting pretty thick," I said. "Maybe you should wait on my boat for it to clear."

"It'll clear up once we get away from the river," he said. "We'll be fine, but what about you?"

"I need some sleep," I said. "Then we can figure out our next move. Let's talk later this morning."

"They're planning to sell the manuscript sometime today or tomorrow," he reminded me.

"I know. But I can't function right now."

He shrugged. "Your call. I'm at the point where I almost don't give a damn about the manuscript."

"Me too," I said under my breath as he got into the car and started it. As they drove away I realized that the whole thing was becoming very personal.

Reaching inside my pocket I took great comfort from the cold touch of the pistol. There would be no more endangering my cousin, or Roy, or Cathy. I might be tired, but it was time to deal with Fish and Rusty. And I was going to do it by myself, and in my own way.

Chapter 21

It began to rain, the temperature was climbing, and I knew that the warmer air, combined with the misty drizzle, would soon eat away the fog. My footsteps rang out on the dock like little muffled thunderclaps in the thick air, and after a moment I became aware of a faint secondary echo that didn't quite match the beat of my walk.

The hairs on the back of my neck stood on end and I stopped. Slipping my right hand into my pocket, I closed it around the grip of the automatic.

Spinning on my toes I crept back in the direction I'd come from. I just managed to stop short of drawing the pistol as Cajun Bob appeared out of the fog. He wore a maroon jogging suit, and had a cigarette in one hand, and an oversized mug of coffee in the other. He was studying his feet as he walked and talking to himself, unaware that he was not alone.

I let out a slow breath, eased my hand out of my pocket and said, "What are you doing up this early, Bob."

He jumped, swung his coffee mug in a defensive motion toward my face, and almost fell as he tried to step back away from me. "Jesus, Wes. You 'bout scared the shit right out of me."

I chuckled. "Sorry. I guess we were both taken by surprise."

"No shit." He took a long swig of coffee, sucked some smoke into his lungs, and then flicked the butt into the river. "This place is like Grand Central Station this morning."

"What do you mean?" I asked.

"Rusty was here not ten minutes ago. Looking for you."

I slid my hand back around the grip of the gun, cocked my head away from Cajun Bob, and listened for any movement around us. Drawing comfort from the fact that the fog was beginning to disperse and it was unlikely that I would stumble into Rusty, I asked, "Is he still around?"

"Nah. He walked up and down the dock for a few minutes, and when he couldn't find you he came back up this way. Then he took off in his boat."

"In this soup?" I asked.

Cajun Bob took another sip of coffee, and then dumped the dregs into the river, shaking the cup as if for emphasis. "I told him he should wait 'til the fog lifts. Said he has a good chart plotter and radar so he wasn't worried. Besides, he was just going up the river a couple hundred yards and was going to drop an anchor and hang on the hook until daylight."

"Thanks," I said, and backed away from him. With my hand resting on the gun in my pocket, I turned and walked down to my boat. The fact that Rusty was searching for me had me pissed off. I had put myself in the role of hunter and I didn't like this reversal. Expecting Fish to materialize at any moment had me on edge. I pulled the gun from my pocket and walked with it held at my side.

I jumped at a sudden movement in front of me and the haunting cry of the startled heron had me lifting the gun. Cold shivers of excitement racked my body as I stepped onto my boat. I felt like I was living on the edge of a well honed knife.

The fog was still thick, so I made a circuit of the upper deck before climbing into the cockpit. My mind seemed in tune with every creak of the dock, every lap of water against the pilings.

I had taken to locking my boat after being surprised by Fish and I was relieved to find the padlock intact. I willed my shoulders to relax, opened the lock, and pulled out the hatch boards.

I should have been happy to be back on board my own boat. I should have been ready to crawl into bed. I was neither. Instead, I began to lay out my plans for going after Rusty and Fish.

After what had happened to Cathy, I decided to go on the offensive. If *Carpe Diem* was anchored nearby, I'd find her, board her, and confront Rusty and Fish. If I were lucky, it would all happen before they knew what hit them.

Keeping the gun within easy reach, I stripped off my damp clothes and pulled on a pair of heavy, dark sweatpants, a matching sweatshirt, and my rain jacket.

I grabbed a bottle of Captain Morgan and took a stiff swig, then moved to the cupboard and dug out my dive knife and its scabbard. I had never killed a man with a knife, but double armed was double prepared. If someone had to die today, it wasn't going to be me.

With the blade strapped to my right calf, I headed back out into the cockpit. Closing up the boat I gathered my thoughts and paused to look around. The beauty that surrounded me as the fog dissipated was breathtaking.

I was very aware of the night sounds of the marina. The occasional early morning car on the parkway. The soft lap of the tide against the dock. The snap of a flag in the freshening breeze. In another time, another place, I would have basked in the peacefulness of it all.

Instead, I climbed over the side of the boat, boarded my dinghy, and grabbed the oars. The motor was out of the question. The noise would carry too far in the quiet of the morning.

A sense of exhilaration was building inside of me as I untied the boat and pushed off into the river. The wind, blowing from the south, helped to carry me out into the middle of the river. It was a struggle to keep the dinghy pointed up river as the current and the tide fought my every stroke. The only thing that made it possible for me to row was the quickening breeze at my back, and my determination to force a showdown.

By the time I'd traversed the length of a football field, the fog had thinned enough so that I could make out the outline of my boat. Another few minutes of rowing, and a quick glance over my shoulder revealed Rusty's trawler. It gave the illusion of having been cast adrift among the clouds.

Exhaustion set in as I pulled the dinghy up to the transom. The strain of rowing and the wear and tear of too many nights without enough sleep left me weary. Tying off to the swim ladder, I leaned back against the rubber tubes of the dinghy and took several deep breaths. I needed to clear my mind and revitalize myself before I could take on Rusty and Fish.

The scent of burning diesel fuel and the soft vibration of *Carpe Diem's* generator were heavy in the air. A helicopter moved over the bay and the deep bellow of a ship's foghorn broke the stillness of the night.

The rain began to fall harder turning the fog into patchy apparitions. I could hear no one stirring on the boat so I reached up and grabbed the ladder.

I figured I had a good chance of getting aboard unseen. From my previous search I knew Rusty's bedroom was in the front of the boat and the flybridge was on the upper deck.

I inched my way up the ladder, swung my leg over the rail and stepped into the cockpit where I tripped over something large and pliable.

I stumbled back to my feet as a large spotlight snapped on, blinding me. As I turned my head away from the light I saw what I'd tripped over. Fish Conners.

A gaping gouge oozed above his ear and a trail of blood ran down his face. The rain turned the blood into a pink stream that flowed along the deck to the cockpit drain. I thought he was dead, and then he let out a loud groan.

"I've been expecting you," Rusty said from up above. The light shifted and fixed on Fish's face. "I'm afraid Fish got a little greedy."

I looked up and tried to see where he was standing, but the bright spot shifted and once again I was blinded as the light hit my face.

I raised my left hand to shield my eyes and moved the right to the butt of my gun. "Bodies are starting to pile up, Rusty."

"You'll be dead before you can get that gun out," Rusty said. "As you said, the bodies are piling up. One more won't make a difference to me."

"Fog's lifting," I said. "People are starting to move about on shore."

"I have another proposition for you, Wes. But first I need for you to get rid of the gun. I want you to take it out very slowly and drop it overboard. Or I can shoot you and dump your body with Fish's."

Rusty held the upper hand again, so I pulled out the gun and held it in front of me.

"Okay," he said. "Now reach out until your hand is over the water, and then drop the gun. I want to hear it splash."

As I dropped the gun overboard I couldn't help but wonder how Roy was going to react to my losing another of his guns.

Rusty interrupted my thoughts. "I didn't hear anything."

"It was a small gun."

"Let me see your hands," he said.

199

I held my hands out in front of me and then jumped as something hit the deck next to where I was standing. It made a dull, hollow thump as it hit, and I looked down as Rusty trained the light on a half empty roll of duct tape resting against Fish's leg.

"Use that on Fish," he said. "I have a feeling that neither of us will be very happy if he wakes up. I'd just as soon not have to worry about him coming after me."

Dropping to one knee I snatched up the tape, and using my teeth pried the edge from the roll. My scalp itched and I had visions in my mind of a giant target painted on my back. The idea that Rusty might shoot me where I kneeled spurred me on and I wrapped several layers of tape around Fish's wrists before moving down to his feet.

The man's legs were monstrous and I was only able to put two wraps around them before the roll of duct tape came to an end. Tossing the empty spool to the side I rose to my feet and turned back to face Rusty as Fish began to stir at my feet.

"Done," I said, turning away from Fish.

"Good. Now, haul your ass up the ladder. Keep your hands in sight, and when you get up here, move to the back of the deck and sit down on the bench seat. If you try anything, I'll shoot you. If you call out, I'll shoot you. Hell, if you make me nervous I'll shoot you."

The metal steps were wet and slippery. As I started to climb, my foot slid and my shin banged hard against the next step, making a dull ringing sound in the night. I cursed, and continued to pull myself upward. Rusty scurried away from the edge of the stair and flashed the light back into my face. With exaggerated care I felt my way along the deck rail to the seat.

"Now what?" I asked.

"Now we have to make a decision," Rusty said. "The man I'm selling the manuscript to is not a pleasant person. I know him from some past business dealings. He's not above trying to take the book away from me. I was counting on Fish to be my backup."

As he spoke, Rusty got busy. He turned on a set of deck lights, set down the spotlight, and without turning his back to me started the boat's engine. He then switched on the windlass, and as the anchor chain was dragged up from the water it made a loud rattling sound that reminded me of an angry castle ghost in an old B movie.

"Let me get this straight, Rusty. Are you suggesting that I be your backup?"

"The thought has crossed my mind."

"And given what's happened over the last few days, what makes you think either of us can trust the other?" I asked. I was dumbfounded at the suggestion and couldn't wait to see how he was going to rationalize this decision.

"It's not a question of trusting each other." Rusty set the gun down on the pilot's seat and with his back to the control panel swung the wheel and turned the boat. A couple of minutes later we passed under the Dauphin Island Parkway Bridge and headed out into Mobile Bay. "I have the gun, and the fact that I haven't killed you will have to be enough for you. The alternative is I kill you, here and now."

"Maybe if you'd put the gun away I'd feel differently." I slid my feet underneath my body and pushed myself up from the seat. Nudging my foot a step toward him, I asked a question that must have been on his mind. "After all that's happened, how can you possibly trust me? I know I don't trust you."

Rusty grabbed the gun and pointed it at me. He appeared to be deep in thought as he swung the boat around the number seven buoy and pushed the throttle forward.

"I have a plan," Rusty said.

"So far your plans have not turned out very well," I pointed out. "And everyone who gets roped into your plan eventually turns up dead. I'm not sure I can afford to join you in your plan."

"Just hear me out," Rusty said. "If you don't like the plan, I can always shoot you."

He had a point. "I guess it doesn't hurt to listen," I said.

"All right, here's the deal, Wes. I have a digital camera that I keep up here to take pictures of fish I catch. I'm going to let you toss Fish's body out into the bay while I take your picture. For insurance purposes, if you know what I mean. I'll also throw in what I promised Fish."

Chapter 22

t was brilliant in its simplicity, and I could only see one problem with his plan. "What's to keep you from using the pictures to blackmail me out of my share of the money?" I asked.

"I'll let you take pictures of me shooting Fish before you toss him over," Rusty said. "We'll have each other by the balls. We've got a couple more hours before we'll be where I want to dump the body, so sit back and relax. After that we'll head to the rendezvous where we swap the book for the money."

"How much are we talking?" I asked.

"Twenty-five grand."

"Plus the ten you promised me earlier," I said.

"I can live with that. But don't get too greedy or you'll be joining Fish with the fishes." Rusty chuckled at his weak joke. He set the autopilot and took a seat where he could shift his attention between me, and the bay before him.

I watched Rusty for several minutes trying to gauge whether I had a chance to get the gun away from him. As I waited he reached for the wheel, swung it to the left and then back again. Something hit the side of the boat with a sharp jolt and I jumped to my feet.

"Just a log in the water," he said. "I didn't see it in time to avoid it. There's a lot of shit out here. They must have had some storms up river."

I eased back into my seat. It seemed Rusty was more alert than I was. Since I had no intention of helping him kill Fish or sell the manuscript, I decided to try to rest until we got to where we were going. I'd look for an opportunity to get the gun then. I took one final look around the boat, leaned back in the chair, and drifted off to sleep.

The damn spotlight tracking across my face woke me. A thin red line was spreading across the horizon, and the stars were fading from the sky. Behind us, the glowing crescent of the moon appeared to be nestled on the bay.

A thumping below where I sat told me that Fish was also awake. Stretching, I stifled a yawn. "I'm getting pissed off about that light in my eyes."

Rusty shifted the light a little to my left and I caught a glimpse of his gun pointing in my direction. "We're about an hour away from our rendezvous. It's decision time, Wes. Either you're with me, or you're with Fish."

"Does Fish know what you're planning?" I asked. Beneath me the pounding grew in intensity and I figured that if Fish didn't know, he suspected.

"No more questions. We need to get rid of Fish before it gets light."

"I'm stiff as hell, Rusty," I said. I stretched once again, this time grabbing my ankles and pulling my shoulders and head toward the floor. "But I'm with you." When I bent forward I reached up my pant leg with my right hand and palmed the dive knife, tucking it up my sleeve as I stood and walked over to the stairs.

I looked at Rusty and gauged my chances. There was maybe four feet separating us and I knew this was as close as I was likely to get to him. He let the pistol hang in one hand and held up a camera in the other. I was pretty sure he could raise the gun faster than I could strike with the knife.

"Do we have to kill him?" I asked.

Rusty slapped the automatic against his leg, and then did it again. Before I could do anything he jumped up and moved toward me with his gun pointed at my gut. At this range there was no way he could miss, and I couldn't defend myself. "Get down there," he said.

As I started down the steps Rusty swung the gun over the railing and fired two shots. Before I could move, he had me covered again.

Below, Fish Conners had gone still.

"So much for matching incriminating pictures," I said.

"It's not a problem." He held out the camera and pointed the gun down the steps. "We'll go down below and while I point the gun at Fish, you can take the damn picture. We'd better get a move on. It will be light soon."

I continued down the steps. When I reached the bottom I looked up and waited. He started to follow me down, paused, and shifted the gun away from me. As he searched for a handhold, I slid the knife from my sleeve and lashed out at his leg. I caught him in the calf and felt the tip of the blade scrape against bone. Rusty let out a yell that sounded more like a battle cry than a sob of pain, and warm blood dripped on my hand.

Rusty kicked out with his good leg and caught me on the side of the head, stunning me. At the same time he dragged himself upward. I shook myself and made a half-hearted grab for the hilt of the knife. My hand was slippery with his blood and the blade slipped from my grasp and fell to the floor before bouncing out of sight.

I crept up the steps, listening for any sounds from Rusty. When I poked my head through the opening I saw that he had moved over to the far side of the boat. His hip rested on the rail and he was twisting his belt around his bleeding leg with one hand and pointing the gun at me with the other.

"I should have killed you right away," he said, raising the gun. There was no way he could miss.

I was thrown off my feet when something big hit the boat, passed under the hull, and hit the propeller. When I looked up Rusty was gone, tossed over the rail by whatever had hit us.

I jumped to my feet, ran to the control console, and shut off the autopilot. As I eased back on the throttle I glanced over the side and tried to spot Rusty. No luck.

The sky was a palette of red and purple and the edge of the sun was just becoming visible as I turned the wheel and went back to search for him. A large tree trunk about a foot in diameter with a tangle of roots shot to the surface off the port side of the boat. I spotted a gaping cut in the bark where the prop had hit, but no Rusty.

I made a half dozen passes around the tree trunk, driving the boat in ever-widening circles. Once again, I failed to find Rusty or his body. When I'd convinced myself I wasn't going to find him, I turned the boat in the direction we had been headed earlier. I set the auto pilot, slowed to near idle speed, and went below.

Fish's unseeing eyes were open. Stepping over his body, I moved into the cabin. I wondered if the manuscript was cursed. How many men had died for this book before my grandfather took possession? Would Rusty be the last?

The manuscript was hidden in the same drawer where I'd found it earlier. It was wrapped in several plastic bags and nestled under the same pair of jeans. I grabbed the book and headed for the main salon where I stopped at the chart table and spent several minutes figuring out where I was headed.

We were a couple of miles from a small cove listed as Prince Cove, just off the Intracoastal Waterway. I figured that if I took my dinghy into the cove, I could call Roy and have him drive over and pick me up.

Entering the cove, I was glad to see that there were no other boats anchored there. I chose a spot not far from the shore and lowered the anchor. As soon as I had *Carpe Diem* secured, I pulled out my phone and called Roy. When he answered, I filled him in on what had happened, emphasizing the dilemma I was in.

"I'm on my way," he said. "Take me maybe an hour to get there."

"I'm taking my dinghy into shore. I see a boat ramp and the road. I'll meet you there."

"I know where it is. Do you want me to call the police?"

I looked down at Fish's body and said, "No. I'll explain when you get here."

I hung up and ran below. I'd seen a hand held VHF radio sitting on a shelf over the navigation table when I was checking my position. I turned it on, switched it to the local weather channel and was relieved when the mechanical voice of the announcer came in loud and clear. I could use it to notify the Coast Guard of *Carpe Diem's* location after Roy picked me up. Sticking the radio in my sweatshirt pocket, I pulled out my handkerchief and began wiping down the boat for fingerprints.

It was full blown daylight by the time I was ready to leave. As an afterthought, I took a minute to grab a fishing pole out of the rack near where Fish's body lie. It had a small lure already attached, and I hoped that if I ran into anyone I could use the fishing pole as my excuse for being out on the water so early in the morning.

I climbed into the dinghy and untied the two registration boards and tucked them under the seat. I didn't want anyone to be able to identify my dinghy. Finally, I drew my sweatshirt hood around my face and reached out to start the motor.

Maybe it was because I was nervous and not paying attention, perhaps it was the cold morning air drifting across the water, or God playing a joke on me, but the outboard refused to start.

I fiddled with the choke, primed the bulb, and pulled the starting cord over and over, all to no avail. Running out of patience, I tilted the prop out of the water, and began rowing toward the distant shore. In my haste, I knocked the fishing pole overboard. So much for excuses, I thought.

Despite the cold, I was sweating by the time I pulled the inflatable onto the beach. Sunshine sparkled on the near still water and a gull circled the beach above me. His lonesome call seemed to mock me as I looked at my watch and realized that I still had at least a half an hour left before I could expect Roy.

Dragging the boat along the sand, I managed to push and pull it up to, and behind a clump of trees. I disconnected the motor from the gas tank, pulled it off the inflatable, tucked the book under my shirt, and deflated the dinghy.

I stumbled over to a piece of log on the westerly edge of the beach and sat down to wait for Roy.

I was beginning to appreciate this southern family more and more. If not for Roy, I'd be stuck not three hundred yards from *Carpe Diem* and Fish Conners' bullet riddled body.

The mind is a well-trained trickster, especially when loaded with guilt and anxiety. The guilt was a byproduct of my Catholic upbringing. The anxiety was something I'd acquired working as a P.I.

There are certain facts you live with when you're out there chasing the shit-heads that have overrun our cities. Number one is that the laws are rigged in their favor. Number two is that if something you've anticipated doesn't go wrong, there's always the unanticipated to look forward to.

The unanticipated was the arrival of a large motor yacht. The day was bright and still, and I heard it before I saw it. By the time it poked its nose into the calm waters of the cove I had carried the motor and gas tank over to the edge of the road. I ran back to the dinghy and half dragged, half carried it halfway to where I'd left everything else. I stopped and watched the yacht motor to within a hundred feet of *Carpe Diem* and begin to let out its anchor.

I estimated it to be in the eighty-foot size range. As I watched, two men appeared on the deck and began lowering an inflatable into the water.

Taking the VHF radio from my pocket I turned it on and tuned it to channel sixteen in time to hear the query, "*Carpe Diem*, this is *Winds Low*. Do you copy?"

I cursed at my luck. It had to be the buyers looking for Rusty, and I didn't want anything to do with them. Just as I was wondering if they had seen me, my phone rang. I grabbed it, but a tall stick figure dressed in a yellow rain jacket looked up and seemed to be studying the beach.

He pointed in my direction as I answered the phone. "I hope you're nearby."

"I'm about three minutes away," Roy said.

The dinghy was in the water now and the man who had pointed at me climbed in to join the first two. The engine roared to life and they headed for *Carpe Diem* at a fast clip.

"I've got company," I said, "and I don't think they're friendly."

As if to confirm my fears the inflatable stopped just long enough at the side of *Carpe Diem* for two of the men to climb out. The third, the man in the yellow jacket, gunned the engine as soon as his partners were on the boat and headed for the beach.

Grabbing my own rolled up dinghy I flung it to my shoulder and with short, lumbering steps began to run to where I'd left the engine.

"Hey," Yellow Jacket called out across the water. "Hey, I want to talk to you."

Ignoring the man's hail, I pushed myself for speed just as Roy pulled up in Jessica's car. It ground to a stop alongside where I'd left my outboard and Roy jumped out. He was loading the motor when a sharp crack filled the air.

A bullet slammed into the side of my dinghy with enough force to knock it from my shoulder, carrying me to the ground with it. Three more gunshots echoed across the water and I scrambled behind a tree.

Out of the corner of my eye I saw Roy reach into the trunk. He grabbed two pistols, spun around, and came running toward me like a two-fisted gunfighter, squeezing off two shots with each gun toward the dinghy.

Peering out from behind the tree, I watched Yellow Jacket swing the inflatable around and head back toward *Carpe Diem*.

"You missed," I said.

"On purpose. I don't want to kill anyone. Now let's get the hell out of here." He handed me the guns and picked up my dinghy with an easy jerk that I found humbling. I followed as he carried it over to the back of the car, where he shoved it in next to the outboard. As he fought to close the trunk, I took the VHF radio from my pocket.

"What are you up to?" he asked.

"Go ahead and get into the car," I said. "Be ready to get the hell out of here. The shit's about to hit the fan."

Once Roy was behind the wheel I hit the send button and spoke into the radio. "Mayday, Mayday, Mayday. Coast Guard this is *Carpe Diem*. We are currently located at Prince Cove and are under attack. I repeat, under attack. Shots have been fired and my crewman has been shot."

I released the send button and heard, "*Carpe Diem, Carpe Diem*, this is the Coast Guard, please repeat." There was a pause and then, "*Carpe Diem,* this is the Coast Guard. We have your position at Prince Cove, if this is correct, please repeat."

"Did you have to call a Mayday? I heard they get too many of those. Big fine too."

"Roy, they were shooting real bullets at me and they had no idea who I was. Not to mention that there's a dead body on board. I kind of think that's an emergency."

"Rusty?"

"Fish," I said, giving him a brief rundown of what had happened.

"You get the manuscript?" he asked.

"I did."

Roy floored the car. "Then let's get the hell out of here."

"I'm not sure it was worth it," I said. "Rusty and Fish are dead and Cathy may never be able to enter her boat in the dark again. Still, I guess the outcome beats the alternative."

"What's that?" Roy asked.

"We could be the dead ones."

If he had a comeback, I didn't hear. I dropped off to la-la land.

Chapter 23

When we got to the marina I held out the manuscript to Roy.

"I talked this over with Jessica. We both think you should be the one to give it to Ma," Roy said.

I hesitated, and then tucked it back beneath my sweatshirt. "When?"

Roy chuckled. "I'm sure Jessica will call and let you know."

I felt myself flush. I had no doubt Jessica would be calling. It was one of the reasons I wanted to get rid of the book. I needed to get out of Mobile—quick.

I climbed out of the car and turned back to face Roy. "Can you do me a favor," I asked.

"What do you need?"

"Can you hang on to my dinghy and motor for a few days. I don't have the energy to worry about it right now."

"Long as you need," he said. "You take care now, you hear?"

I nodded and felt a twinge of loss as he pulled away. I realized I was going to miss my uncle and wondered if he'd be interested in going for a sail before I left Mobile.

As I made my way to my boat I felt as if I'd just run a marathon. My legs hurt. My back hurt. My head hurt. Hell, I couldn't think of a damn thing on me that didn't hurt.

It took three tries to get the lock open and I stumbled twice walking down the steps to the main salon. A shower was out of the question. I'd never make it back down the dock. Instead, I shucked my clothes, tucked the manuscript under the settee, and climbed up into the front berth.

I slept the sleep of the dead for twenty hours. I don't know if it was the too few fitful hours of sleep I'd been able to sneak in since my cousin Jessica had come into my life, or the fact that my body had used up every ounce of adrenaline it had produced the previous week. Whatever it was, a bomb could have gone off next to the boat and I wouldn't have noticed.

When I awoke I peeked out the port window next to where I slept. The sun was shining, and several fishing boats drifted nearby. Shorts and t-shirts appeared to be the dress of the day and one of the boaters even had his shirt off. I smiled in anticipation of warm weather. Hell, that was the reason I'd come south.

I climbed down from the front berth, drew on a pair of cargo shorts, and went to check on the manuscript. Even though Rusty and Fish were dead, my heart raced and my hands felt a little clammy as I reached under the cushion. I half expected the book to be gone. When my fingers touched the plastic bag surrounding it, I relaxed.

I was surprised Jessica hadn't called yet. Then again, maybe she had. I picked up my phone and sure enough, there were eight messages from Jessica.

I decided my cousin could wait. After brushing my teeth I put on a pot of coffee, scrambled half a dozen eggs with cheese, and sat down to eat. The phone rang. Pushing aside my plate I reached for the phone and felt relieved when I saw that it was not Jessica.

"Hey," I said. "How ya doing?"

"I'm better," Cathy said. "Can I come on down to your boat?"

"Can you give me an hour or so? I guarantee you don't want to see me before I've showered. I can't even stand myself right now."

"See you then." She hung up and I dove into my eggs.

I refilled my coffee mug, gathered up my bathroom bag, a towel, and a change of clothing, and was headed out the door when the phone rang again. I knew who it had to be, and as much as I wanted a hot shower I couldn't leave her hanging. I set my things on the cockpit seat, stepped back into the boat and picked up my phone.

"Didn't you get my messages," she asked.

"Good morning to you too," I said.

"I was beginning to think you were dead."

"Just dead tired. And now all I want to do is take a shower. I feel like I spent the night mud wrestling."

"Uncle Roy said you got the manuscript back."

"When do you want to pick it up?"

"How about dinner tonight? It's just after noon now. Let's meet at the marina restaurant at six. Gran's looking forward to meeting you. And by the way, she doesn't know you've got the book. It will be a nice surprise for her."

216

"Me too," I said. My heart did a strange triple beat and my hand started to shake a little. I felt uneasy about meeting her for the first time.

Jessica didn't give me a chance to change my mind. She laughed, said something I couldn't understand, and hung up the phone.

As I walked down the dock toward the showers my mood turned dark. The muscles in my neck and back felt bunched, like a tangle of taught banjo strings waiting to break.

Cajun Bob sat by himself at the gathering table when I rounded the dock house. He was dressed in shorts and a Guy Harvey t-shirt, and was reading the paper while sipping from a large coffee mug. Any thoughts I had of slipping into the showers unnoticed were put to rest when he looked up and waved me over.

"Have you heard what happened to Rusty?" he asked.

It was an unexpected question that turned my knees to spaghetti and threatened to steal my composure. I grabbed a chair, leaned on it a moment for support, then pulled it out and sat down. I shook my head and waited, afraid my voice would betray me if I said anything.

Bob laid his paper on the table, pushed it aside and leaned toward me. "Son of a bitch just disappeared. The police seem to think he's dead."

"What happened?"

Bob shook his head and picked up his coffee cup. "You know, I never did believe those stories they used to tell around here about him. Shit, if I'd a known, I'd have been a little less flip with the man."

"Bob, what the hell happened?"

"I've got a friend, Buddy Jenkins. He's with the Coast Guard. I ran into him at Wal-Mart this morning. We're on the same bowling team, you know, and…."

I reached across the table and grabbed his wrist as he began to raise his coffee cup toward his mouth. "I don't need the long version, Bob." My voice reverberated across the table and Bob gave me an irritated look. "Just tell me, what happened to Rusty?"

This time he shot me a startled look. "Oh yeah, you guys were getting sorta friendly. First time I…."

"Bob."

"Right, Rusty. They think he might have been running drugs. The Coasties figure maybe he tried to double cross someone and it got him and some other guy killed."

"Come again?" I said. I couldn't believe what I was hearing and it must have showed on my face.

"Yeah," he continued. "I never would have thought it either. They found Rusty's boat with a dead man on board. Buddy didn't know the dead guy's name. Guy was shot twice and there was no sign of Rusty. They stopped another boat and they had something like half a million dollars cash on board. Some guys from Venezuela, here illegally. They aren't talking of course. They demanded that they be allowed to talk to their consulate or some shit like that. Don't you just love these people who come to our country and try to use our laws against us?"

"And they found drugs?" I asked, ignoring his diatribe.

"No. According to Buddy there wasn't a trace around. They think he either hid them while trying to cut a better deal for himself, or he never had them and was going to hijack the cash. Either way it got him and the other guy killed."

"Doesn't the drug trade run the other way?" I asked. "I mean, they come in from South America and someone buys the goods up here."

"So maybe it went the other way and they hijacked the money from Rusty. What difference does it make? He's just as dead one way or the other. I'm just repeating the story as I heard it."

"If they didn't find the body, how do you know Rusty's dead?"

"Hey, these are drug people we're talking about. They probably cut him up into little pieces and fed him to the gators. These guys don't play around, man. They play for keeps."

I stood and nodded toward the showers. "I guess you're right. I've got to get cleaned up. I'll talk to you later."

"Sure." Cajun Bob drained his coffee cup, made a face, and asked, "Did he ever find you the other night?"

"No." I turned away from him so he couldn't see the worried look on my face. "I haven't seen him in a couple of days."

"Just be glad he didn't drag you into this shit," he said. "You might be swimming with the fishes yourself right now."

"Yeah," I said, as I headed toward the showers. "I'm damn glad that didn't happen."

While I showered I gave some thought to what had happened to Rusty's body. There was a better than average chance that it was wedged among debris somewhere along the bottom of Mobile Bay. I wished the whole thing would go away, but it wasn't likely. I suspected that sometime in the next couple of weeks some fisherman out on the bay would find the body. Then the whole episode would crop up in the news again.

I just hoped that Cajun Bob hadn't mentioned me to his Coast Guard friend, or said anything about Rusty looking for me the day he disappeared.

When I got back to the boat I poured a cup of coffee and moved out into the cockpit to wait for Cathy. I had mixed emotions about her visit. I liked her, but something I'd seen in her over the last few days had tempered my enthusiasm toward our relationship.

Then there was Jessica. I didn't want to admit to myself that I was developing feelings for her. It was a forbidden relationship, a place I would never allow myself to go. Still, I couldn't deny the attraction.

I put aside my musings when I caught sight of Cathy strolling down the dock. She had nice legs and looked good in her blue shorts and loose-fitting white blouse. As she approached a breeze came up and tousled her hair.

"Come aboard," I said. I held out my hand and helped her down into the cockpit, then added, "We can go below if you'd like?"

"It's nice out here." She dropped my hand, plopped down on the seat, and leaned back.

"Coffee? Coke?"

She shook her head and I sat down opposite her. I was unsure of what to say, unsure of what she wanted. After several awkward moments she pointed over my shoulder. "Looks like that guy caught something out there."

I twisted around and watched an elderly man with a gray beard, kinky white hair and caramel colored skin reel in about a three-pound speckled trout.

"Nice catch," I called out.

"Third one just like it," he said.

He took the fish off the line and tossed it into a Styrofoam icebox, and I turned back to find Cathy studying me.

"Did you hear about Rusty?" I asked.

She nodded and licked her lips. "I ran into Cajun Bob on my way over. It's all he could talk about. Was the dead man they found Fish?"

"I don't know," I said. "Seems likely. I guess you don't have to worry about them anymore. There might be some questions though."

"What do you mean?"

"The police might come around, asking questions about Rusty."

"I don't know anything. I barely knew the man. I'm certainly not going to file kidnapping charges against a dead man."

"That's good," I said. "I'd just as soon not have to explain the whole situation to the police."

She shot me a look, and I wasn't sure if it was fear or loathing I read in her eyes. "You have anything to do with this, Wes?"

I shook my head. "Cajun Bob told me it was drug related."

"We both know that's not true, don't we?" she said. "You don't have to worry though, I won't say anything. Besides, I'm going back to Wisconsin."

"With what's his face?" I asked.

She smiled for the first time since climbing aboard. "No, not with what's his face. I sent him packing. The son of a bitch admitted he was late getting down here because of some woman he met. Tried to justify it by reminding me how long he was in jail and how long he had to do without. Said she didn't mean a thing. I didn't much care."

"When you leaving?"

"Couple of days." She stood and stretched, and then gazed out over the water. "I'm going to miss this place."

"So stay," I said.

"I can't. I'm staying in a motel until I can get everything off the boat, then it goes up for sale."

"I'm sorry," I said.

"Don't be." She reached out and touched my arm. "I've got to go."

I had nothing else to say. Apparently, neither did Cathy. She gave me a quick peck on the cheek and then turned and climbed off the boat.

I watched her until she disappeared around the corner of the dock house and felt a twinge of sadness as I headed inside. We'd had something together, even if it was only for a short time. I took a beer out of the fridge, hesitated, and then popped the top. It was a little after three, earlier than I usually drank. I figured what the hell. Sometimes you've just got to go with the mystical teachings of Parrothead philosophy. After all, it really is five o'clock somewhere.

Chapter 24

I downed a second beer and turned my thoughts to the upcoming meeting with my grandmother. I paced back and forth in the cabin. Three short steps forward, three short steps back, then I'd reach for the phone, determined to cancel dinner. Every time I dialed the number, I hung up before it could ring through. Then I'd step out into the cockpit to clear my head.

It was a ritual I repeated a dozen times or more, chastising myself over and over for being such a coward. The idea of meeting the woman my father called mother terrified me, even though I knew this was as close as I was ever likely to get to knowing my father.

My skin started to itch and I half expected welts to form on my arms and legs. I hated feeling that I was out of control.

I took a deep breath and forced myself to sit, but I was back on my feet within moments. It felt as if six o'clock would never arrive.

Finally, it was time to go. I grabbed my wallet, climbed off the boat, and trudged along the dock like an old bull on its way to the hamburger mill.

When I reached the parking lot Jessica's car was nowhere in sight. I felt a mixture of relief and irritation that they weren't there. My first inclination was to head up to the bar for another beer while I waited for them. Instead, I headed over to the round table where I took a seat to await my fate.

They were ten minutes late. Roy climbed out first, and when he opened the passenger door Jessica's father, Ben, followed. Ben wore black slacks and shirt along with his clerical collar and I couldn't remember if that was how he'd dressed the last time I met him. At some point Jessica joined him, but my attention was on the woman Roy was helping out of the car.

Tiny and fragile looking, she had short thin white hair and carried an oversized black purse that looked almost like a suitcase in her small hands. Her navy skirt hung down to her ankles. A white blouse, and a dark blue sweater that didn't quite match the color of her skirt hung on her as if she'd lost a good deal of weight. It reminded me that Jessica had told me she'd been ill.

Roy took her arm and led her over to me while Jessica and her father joined us. I thought I read the same apprehension in my grandmother's eyes that I felt. As I steeled myself for my first contact with my grandmother, I wondered if she had the same fears I had.

She halted before me, released Roy's arm, and held out her hand. "Hello, Wes. I've been looking forward to meeting you."

As I took her hand I almost laughed at the formality of her greeting. I hesitated, then dropped her hand and gave her a gentle hug.

She looked up and I saw tears in her eyes. I smiled down at her, and she threw her arms around my waist, clutching me to her.

"I'm so sorry Wes. So very sorry."

She smelled of lilacs and mothballs, and her tears left a damp circle on my shirt. "It's all right," I said. I tried to take a small step away from her but she tightened her grip and let out a large sob. It was as if she feared I'd disappear like a wisp of smoke.

"It's not all right." She let me go, sniffed, and pulled away from me. Her pale blue eyes were filled with tears that flowed down her cheeks, cutting tiny rivulets into her makeup. She reached into the pocket of her sweater, took out a tissue, and blew her nose before letting loose an endearing smile.

"I should have stood up to your mother when she suggested it would be best for you," she said.

"It's all right," I repeated. "My mother can be a very convincing woman." If anyone knew that to be true, it was me.

My grandmother put her hands on her hips and glared at me. "Do you think if you say that enough you'll make it okay?" she asked. "I'd like to apologize in my own way if you don't mind."

I liked her feisty attitude. "That's fine with me," I said. Tucking her arm in mine she let me lead her up the stairs and it wasn't until we were entering the restaurant that I remembered the manuscript.

I handed her off to Roy. "I've got to run back to the boat for a minute. Why don't y'all sit down and I'll be right back."

My grandmother laughed and nudged Jessica. "I do believe Wes's southern roots are starting to show," she said.

"What do you mean?" I asked.

"She means you're already y'alling people," Ben said. "It's a sure sign you're from down here, or that you've been here too long."

I'd been so wrapped up in meeting my grandmother I'd forgotten he was there. I nodded at him and smiled at her. "That may be, but if you'll excuse me, I'll be right back."

Turning, I sprinted down the steps and had started off toward the boat at a fast walk when Jessica called out from behind me. "Wait up, Wes."

I slowed and gave her a chance to catch up with me before resuming my trek down the dock. "What's on your mind," I asked.

"I just wanted to let you know that Uncle Roy and I decided not to tell Gran what happened with Rusty and Fish. She'll be eighty-one in May and she's on heart medication."

"I don't have a problem with that. What are we going to tell her?"

"Just that you went to see the lawyer, Sam Quinlin, and that he admitted to taking it. You talked him into giving it back."

"Think she'll buy that story?" I asked.

"I don't see why not," Jessica said.

We had reached the boat and when I started to climb aboard Jessica grabbed my shirt sleeve and pulled me around to face her.

"There's something else we need to talk about," she said.

"What's that?"

Jessica shuffled back and forth on her feet and looked out across the river, avoiding my eyes. "I really like you, Wes."

I groaned inwardly and took a step back. "Look, Jessica, I can't go there."

She shifted her gaze to my face and I thought I caught a flash of anger in her eyes. "Do you really think I'm just some dumb hick?"

"No. I understand things are different around here."

She moved in close to me and I could feel her hot breath on my face. "You're either stupid or an asshole, Wes Darling. I've just been funnin' with you."

"So you're not interested." I said.

She got a funny look on her face, and then she threw her arms around my neck and kissed me. Before I could respond she let go of me and pulled away.

Her eyes sparkled and she smiled. "Oh, I'm interested, Darling. Did you know that in Alabama first cousins can even get married?"

I opened my mouth but before I could find the words to respond Jessica reached out and pressed a hand to my lips. "Don't worry, though, I know I'm too young to get married."

Again I was speechless as Jessica spun around and started walking away from me. She stopped when she was about ten feet away and looked back at me. She grinned, a grin that would have done the Cheshire cat proud.

"What I really came down here to tell you, Darling, is that I'm not your cousin. Daddy adopted me when I was two."

With that final barb Jessica took off running down the dock, leaving me standing there with my mouth hanging open. I almost took off after her, but then I remembered the manuscript.

As I opened up the boat and retrieved the manuscript, I realized that I still had a lot to learn about this new family of mine.

When I stepped back outside I was surprised to find Jessica standing on the pier, leaning against the piling.

Apparently, she was done teasing me. She stretched her arms over her head. "It's so damn beautiful down here on the river," she said. "Do you know how lucky you are?"

"It's why I live on a boat. I can't afford a house or condo on the water. Besides, I like the people I meet living this way. Come on. Let's get this book back to grandmother."

She moved up next to me, tucked her arm in mine, and we strolled arm in arm back to the restaurant. She was quiet until we reached the stairs, then she let go of my arm and looked at me.

"Thanks," she said.

"For what?"

"For getting the manuscript back. For agreeing to meet with Gran. Just for being a part of my life for the past week. It's been nice getting to know you."

It was hard to believe it had only been a week. I felt like I'd known her a lot longer.

"I've enjoyed it too," I said

We joined my grandmother, Roy, and Ben at a table overlooking the river. The three of them were having a heated conversation when we walked up and she didn't seem surprised when I set the wrapped manuscript in front of her.

"I was just explaining to mama how you talked that lawyer into giving the book back to you," Roy said.

"And I was explaining right back to Roy what a basket of manure that story is. I'm old, and maybe a little decrepit, but I'm not senile. I read the papers and I watch television." She lowered her voice to a whisper and stared me in the eyes. "Now tell me the truth Wes. Did you kill that young man?"

"What young man?" I asked.

"That lawyer. Sam Quinlin. I read in the paper how he'd been shot in his office. Police thought it might be a burglary. Now they're trying to tell me you got the book back from him."

"No ma'am," I said. "I didn't kill anyone. I wouldn't have done that to get the book back."

"Good." She pushed the manuscript over to the side of the table as if it was unimportant. "So, why don't we order some dinner? It's on me today."

"You believe me?"

She reached across the table and patted my hand. "Of course I do."

"Don't you want to know what really happened?" I asked.

She looked up at the ceiling, pretended to study the tiles and said, "No. It's obvious the four of you have decided that I shouldn't know, so we'll let it go at that. Now let's order, I'm hungry."

***

The sky was charcoal gray, the air smelled of an approaching storm, and the temperature was falling as a cold front made its way into the area. Standing in the parking lot, watching my newfound family drive away, was a surreal experience. It felt as if I was awakening from a dream.

The most surprising thing to me was the disappointment I felt with their departure. As I turned back toward the docks, I realized that the urge to get into the boat and move on to another location was not quite as strong as it had been just a few days earlier. And I had to admit, the excitement of chasing down the manuscript had been invigorating.

I was grateful that the ordeal with the manuscript was over. Warm feelings toward Jessica washed over me and for the first time I wasn't afraid about what I felt. Life is grand, I thought, and then I turned the corner of the dock house and Rusty Dawson limped out of the shadows.

Chapter 25

Rusty's sudden appearance brought me to a stop. His jeans were torn, his sweatshirt stained and several sizes too large. The muscles around his eyes and mouth sagged. His hair was uncombed and large dark circles rimmed his eyes. He appeared to have aged twenty years.

I back peddled, but before I could turn and run he held up his right hand and showed me the gun.

"I wouldn't," he said. His voice was thick and raspy and he let out a harsh cough. Turning his head to the side he spit into the river. "Where's the book?"

I thought about my frail grandmother who had carefully tucked the book into her purse before leaving the restaurant. I saw the desperate look in Rusty's eyes, took in the way his hand twitched as he held the gun on me, and I said, "I gave it to Roy."

His brow furrowed and he sucked in his lower lip. Extending his arm, Rusty took two steps toward me and pushed the barrel of the gun against my chest.

"Let's go," he said.

"Where?"

"To see your uncle, boy. Where else? I want my book back."

"I don't know where he lives," I said.

"That's too bad." He pushed the barrel a little deeper into my chest. "In that case I don't need you hanging around, do I? I might as well kill you here and go see your grandmother. Or perhaps I'll have a talk with your pretty cousin, Jessica. I'm sure that with a little persuasion one of them will tell me where Roy lives."

"And if I take you there, you'll kill both of us."

"You'd better believe someone's going to die tonight. I got me no reason to be nice. It can be you and Roy. It can be your grandmother and Jessica. I don't really give a damn. I want the book back, and I don't want anyone to know I'm alive. If you can get me the book without Roy knowing about me, maybe you're the only one who'll have to die."

I considered the situation, and then gave a brief nod. "I'll take you to him, but I don't have a car." I was hoping I hadn't just set Roy up for death. I hoped that between now and when we got to his place I'd come up with a plan.

Rusty eased the gun from my chest. "Let's go. I've got a car. And no games, I meant what I said about the women. At this point I don't really care who dies."

As I turned and headed out to the parking lot, I thought about my predicament. There was clearly a tone of despair in Rusty's voice, and I had no reason to believe he wasn't serious with his threats.

"Not so fast," he said.

I slowed my pace. In the quiet of the night I could hear him making little whimpering noises and muttering beneath his breath. I wondered if his ordeal hadn't pushed him over the line that separates sanity from insanity.

When we reached the car, Rusty opened the driver's side door and said, "Get in. Put both hands on the wheel and don't move."

I complied and he opened the rear door. The car rocked and he let out a loud groan as he got situated directly behind me. I looked at him in the mirror. Anger glowed in his eyes and I got the feeling that he would love nothing more than to shoot me.

"You're hurt," I said.

"No shit. You stuck a shiv in my leg and then left me to drown in the middle of Mobile Bay. Under the circumstances, I'd say I'm not doing too badly."

"I looked for you out there. I couldn't find you."

"Close the door and drive." Rusty coughed, opened the window and spit onto the pavement. "I've got the gun pointed dead center against this seat. You so much as sneeze and I'll put a bullet right through you."

"You shoot me while I'm driving and we're both going to die."

"I'm already a dead man. If I get caught I'll either be charged with Fish's murder, or drug trafficking, or both. One thing you'd better understand. I'd rather be dead than spend the last years of my life in prison."

I studied the dark pools of his eyes through the mirror, considered my options and realized I had none. "The road to Roy's place is pretty rough. I wouldn't want that gun to go off by accident," I said.

"Then you'd better drive real slow. Now let's get the hell out of here."

I fought the urge to fling open the door and try to escape, and as I started the car a plan began to form in my mind.

It started to rain as we pulled out of the parking lot, a fine mist that turned into a downpour by the time we reached the parkway.

Beads of sweat formed along my brow and I couldn't get my mind off the gun resting against the back of the driver's seat. Every time we hit a bump I tensed, waiting for the jarring motion that would send a bullet burrowing into my back.

"So how did you get off the bay?" I asked.

"I'm a lot better swimmer than you'd expect for my age. I swim almost every day."

"But I came looking for you."

He laughed. "I figured you were making sure I was dead, so I ducked behind that log we hit. When you left, I hung onto that log and headed off to shore."

"You swam all the way to shore?"

"Never would have made it. I was cold, and I figured I was a goner. That's when I came up on this old guy in a fishing boat. He about peed his pants when I popped up from behind that log. That's where I got these clothes and the car."

"What happened to the fisherman?"

"You can lay that one on your conscience, boy. I did what I had to do to survive."

I didn't ask any more questions after that. If I had any doubts about what he had planned for me, his confession erased them.

By the time we reached the turnoff to the cabin, my entire body felt like a giant spring wound tight and ready to snap. I couldn't think of one reason for Rusty to keep me around beyond this point. It was time to act.

I increased the pressure on the accelerator as we came up to the road leading to Roy's place. It was now or never. When we were almost past the turnoff I slammed on the brakes and swung the wheel to the left hoping that Rusty would be tossed across the back seat.

The tires spun on the gravel, caught, and spun again. I threw open the door, put my hand in front of my face, and dove onto the road. Something popped in my left shoulder sending a sharp spasm of pain through my body. The car careened off into the field, smashing with a shudder against the trunk of a giant pine tree.

Pain washed over me in waves, but I ignored it and forced myself to my feet. I didn't know if Rusty had survived, but I couldn't wait to find out. My left arm hung at my side like a broken wing. I had to reach Roy before Rusty did. Nausea nipped at me as I set off toward the cabin at a painful trot.

Tiny needles of rain lashed my face, and halfway across the grassy field my feet flew out from beneath me. This time when my shoulder popped it sounded to me like the crack of a ship's cannon.

I screamed and lay there, too stunned to move. Cold, sweet smelling rain washed over my body, reviving me. I struggled to my feet, drew several deep-sobbing breaths into my lungs, and ran on. To my left I thought I heard two or maybe three shots. It was too dark to be sure of where I was headed, but to my right there appeared a dark curtain that I hoped was the woods. I swerved and headed toward them.

I never made it. I tripped on a rock or a tree stump, or some other unseen rubble. This time I twisted my body as I fell and took the jarring blow on my right side. Still, the pain roared up in my left shoulder and I passed out.

I awoke with my face buried in a mound of mint smelling leaves. I thought I heard another gunshot, but it could have been distant thunder. Disoriented, I rolled onto my back, let out a groan, and tried to sit up.

Something brushed against my leg and I felt a presence beside me. My heart raced and I gathered what remaining strength I possessed and prepared to make my last stand when Roy's voice sounded in my ear. "What's going on son? You hurt?"

I squinted up at him through the rain, then did a double take and began to pull away.

"Easy there, Wes." He pulled something from his face and leaned forward, once again speaking in a soft voice he added, "Night vision goggles. Didn't think about the effect on someone seeing them. I'm no monster. Now tell me, where are you hurt?"

"I think I dislocated my shoulder. And Rusty's alive. He's armed and out there somewhere. How'd you find me?"

"I heard a crash. Came out to investigate and thought I heard gunshots so I went back inside and got my goggles and a gun. It was Dwayne that found you. Dog's a born tracker."

"What do we do now?" I asked.

"I'm gonna put an end to this nonsense with Rusty once and for all."

"You're not going to just kill him?" I asked.

"Most definitely."

"Roy, I...."

"It's not something that's up for discussion. He's not going to go away and we can't turn him over to the cops. You know damn well he'll drag all of us into this mess if we go to them. I'd like to get you out of the rain, but I need to take care of Rusty first."

I thought about it for a moment and remembered the way Rusty had smiled when he talked about going after my grandmother and cousin.

"You're right," I said.

"I know you don't like this son. I don't like killing either but this is no different than any other war. Sometimes, it's kill or be killed. There are places not far from here where we can dump a body and only the gators are likely to find it. Now I want you to stay put so I know where you are. These goggles help but they only do so much, especially in this rain. The lightning flashes are blinding. I'll leave Dwayne here with you."

Roy stood. Ordering the dog to stay, he slipped away into the night. The rain muffled his footsteps but a staccato burst of lightning strikes made the field seem like a giant ballroom lit by strobe lights. I watched his slow motion progress, watched a shadow step out from behind a tree to his left.

I called out a warning as I pushed myself to my feet. A clap of thunder drowned out my voice. The sky lit up with another series of lightning flashes. I heard the snap of a gunshot and saw Roy fall.

I didn't wait for the next flash. I took off in a stumbling sprint toward him. My left shoulder radiated pain down my arm, but I ignored it.

Dwayne loped alongside me, but something in his canine brain must have registered that his master was in danger and Dwayne took off with a burst of speed.

I had hoped to take Rusty by surprise but he turned his head in my direction as another flash lit the sky. He dropped to one knee, brought up his arm and pointed the gun at me.

The dog flew through the air, but Rusty threw himself to the ground and Dwayne flew by him. Without pause, Rusty swung around and shot the dog.

Roy's pistol was still in his hand. I tried not to look at his bloody head as I reached down and snatched it up. I twisted my shoulder as I jumped to my feet and a wave of dizziness passed over me. Fighting for my life I turned, the gun at my side, only to find that Rusty had me covered.

He said something that was lost in the din of the storm. Another flash of lightning accentuated his skeletal grin. He took a step toward me, raised the gun, and I knew I was about to die.

My shoulder throbbed to the beat of my heart and I was having trouble concentrating. Thunder crashed, another series of bolts lit the sky, and in that split second I saw Dwayne stagger to his feet, lunge forward, and sink his teeth into Rusty's leg.

Rusty opened his mouth and let out a silent scream and swung the gun toward me. I lifted Roy's gun, but Rusty was a fraction of a second quicker. I saw a flash, felt something slam into my left leg, and as I teetered on my good leg I fired twice in his direction. Then I fell to the ground and gave in to the waves of darkness that enveloped me.

Chapter 26

I awoke to find myself lying naked under a heavy blanket. For several moments I wondered where I was. Memories of what had happened flooded my mind and it took me a moment to realize I was in Roy's cabin.

I was lying on his sofa bed, which was opened up in the middle of the room. I had no idea how I had gotten there. No idea what had happened to Roy or Rusty. My shoulder was tightly bound, my leg was bandaged, and I felt as if an iron had seared my nerve endings.

"It's about time you got up."

Twisting my head to the left, I found Jessica sitting on a leather chair that had been moved next to the sofa. She was dressed in yellow pajamas and a white fleece robe and at the moment she looked like an angel. Dwayne was curled up next to her on the floor. His flank was wrapped in a large bandage and when I moved, he looked up. I tried to speak, but all that came out was a harsh, groaning sound.

Jessica lifted a glass off the table next to where she sat. There was a straw in it and she leaned forward and placed the straw between my lips. The water was cool and eased my discomfort. When she started to pull the glass away I clamped my teeth onto the straw and shook my head.

She used a little more force to remove it. "The doctor said a little at a time. Take a couple of good swallows and I'll give you more."

I nodded, followed her directions and croaked out, "More."

This time, she left the straw a little longer. When she finally pulled it away I asked, "Roy?"

"He's all right. The bullet creased his skull. He always did say he had a hard head. He managed to drag you back here. After that he called a doctor and me."

"What about the police?"

"No police."

"But how?" I asked. "You mentioned a doctor. They have to report gunshot wounds."

If she gave a response, I didn't hear it. My mind was growing foggy. I began to drift on medicated currents, and then I was asleep.

The next time I came up for air it was Roy who was seated beside my bed. His head was bandaged, and when he heard me stir he reached over and laid his crossword puzzle on the table.

"How you feeling?" he asked.

"Sore."

"That's not too surprising. In the past week you've been beaten, shot, and had your shoulder dislocated. You're lucky to be young. I haven't gone through half of what you've gone through, and it's all I can do to walk across the cabin."

"I'm just damn glad you're alive. I thought Rusty had killed you. By the way, what happened to him?"

"Your shot was a lot more accurate than his. You killed him dead."

"I guess it was him or me. Why aren't the cops sniffing around?"

"The police don't know about the whole mess."

I frowned. "How's that possible? Jessica said something about a doctor."

"That's a bit of a story." Roy reached for his pipe and tobacco pouch and leaned back in his chair. When he had it going smoothly, he took a deep drag, exhaled, and filled the room with the sweet scent of his tobacco.

Lying back I waited, mesmerized by the thin tendrils of smoke he created as he puffed away on his pipe. I waited while he decided what to tell me. When his pipe died, he let out an audible sigh and studied it for a long time, then placed it on the table and leaned forward in his chair.

"You familiar with the survivalist movement?" he asked.

"Sure. They're a bunch of nuts that have stockpiled food and weapons in preparation for the apocalypse. They're convinced world destruction is just around the corner."

"It's a little more complicated than that, Wes. Many are patriots who believe our government is leading the nation further and further away from the constitution. The doctor is a survivalist and a member of the Southern American Militia. The group's website lists its mission as the preservation of the constitution."

"You a member of this group?"

Roy shook his head and sat back into the chair. "No. Let's just say I have a good many friends in the movement. I certainly think the government's way out of whack. I guess you could call me a constitutionalist."

"Tell me a little more about the doctor."

"He's a member. While I'm ready to give the Congress a little more time to set things right, he'd just as soon dump the current system. His family owned a big plantation before The War for States Rights. He thinks slavery should be reinstated. But he's an old war buddy and I saved his life back in Nam. He won't go to the police."

I looked up at the ceiling and tried to sort it all out. Maybe Jessica hadn't been kidding when she referred to crazy Uncle Roy.

"I'll have to figure out a story for around the marina," I said.

"Jessica took care of that."

I groaned. "Why is it I'm almost as worried about that as the truth?"

Roy let out a deep belly laugh. "It is a little disconcerting to have your life dependant on Jessica, isn't it? Not that she'd do anything to intentionally hurt you. But she does spin a convoluted web when she tells a story. I told her to keep it simple."

The covers were beginning to itch and I pushed them off my chest. "What did she tell them?"

"The truth, what else."

I raised my body and tried to lean on my arm but the shoulder began to ache and I had to lie back down. "That doesn't make me feel any better, Roy."

"She spread the word that you were in an accident and you were staying with family until you recovered a bit."

"What happened to the car?" I asked.

"Had another friend tow it away. Took it to a junk yard where the policy is ask no questions."

"And Rusty?"

"I borrowed a boat and took the body up the Mobile River to a deserted cutoff I know of," he said after awhile. "Daddy used to take me up there to fish when I was a boy. You can't get to it except by boat, and then only if you know how to get in."

"You don't think anyone will find him?"

"Lots of gators out there. Not too many people. I weighed the body down pretty good. Even if they find him someday there won't be much left. No reason for the cops to come looking for us."

He sounded more confident than I felt. I was growing drowsy, and before I could thank him, I dropped back off to sleep.

Epilogue

It was April Fool's Day by the time I got away from Mobile. The temperatures had been slowly rising and after a week of rain the sun was up, there was a nice breeze, and Mobile Bay was as smooth as a sheet of ice.

My shoulder had healed nicely but my leg was still a little stiff. When I first stepped on it in the mornings the nerve endings felt as if they were on fire, but after moving around a little the pain would ease. Roy's doctor friend had given me some medication and a list of exercises. I'd been exercising every day and it seemed to help. I put the medication away and decided I'd only dig it out if the pain became unbearable.

The plan was to cross the bay and take the Intracoastal Waterway to Apalachicola, Florida. From there we'd take three overnight sails, stopping in Clearwater, Ft. Myer's Beach, and ending up in Key West.

As I steered the boat out of Dog River and under the Dauphin Island Parkway Bridge, I heard the phone ring. I ignored it and set my attention to the channel markers up ahead. Ten minutes later, Jessica stepped out of the cabin. She had a cup of coffee in each hand, a smile on her face, and was wearing a Brazilian bikini that would have been ruled indecent in at least half-a-dozen states.

She handed me one of the cups and sat down next to me. "I just got off the phone with Uncle Roy."

"What did he want?"

Jessica took a sip of her coffee and made a face. "The State Department is sending someone to pick up the manuscript. They found the owner. Some abbey in France. He said Gran is anxious to get rid of the thing after all the trouble it's caused."

We sat there and enjoyed the peace and quiet of Mobile Bay. Ten minutes later, she broke my heart. "Uncle Roy also said the confirmation of my summer class schedule came too."

I looked at her out of the corner of my eye. "You don't have to go, you know. There's plenty of room for two on board. It doesn't have to be just a six week trip to the Keys. It's a big world and there's lots of water to sail on. We could spend the summer on the Chesapeake, or in Maine."

Jessica took my hand, turned it up, and ran her thumb across the palm. "And then what? We're too young to be retired. Where's the money going to come from?"

I thought about the stash of diamonds I had hidden in a secret cubby under the front berth. A small fortune I'd recovered a few months earlier when I'd reluctantly tracked down the thief.

"I've got some money put aside," I said.

"I'm not willing to be a kept woman," Jessica said. "Besides, I hated dropping out last semester. I want my degree, but after Granddaddy died and the manuscript was stolen I missed too many classes. If I take summer classes I'll be done by the end of the year."

"Then what?"

"I don't know, Wes. I always thought I'd teach. I don't see myself traveling from port to port never feeling I'm at home."

Jessica let go of my hand and stood up. She looked back toward the Dog River and I knew I wasn't going to win this argument. I gave it one more try. "I thought home was where the heart is."

"It is." She spoke so softly that I barely heard her next words. "My home is Mobile. Can you see yourself settling down there? Buying a house? Having children?"

"Probably not."

Jessica looked down at me. "That's why I never suggested it. You're a wanderer, Wes. A hundred and fifty years ago you would have been heading west or maybe taking a ship to Australia. I like that about you. But it's not for me."

"So what do we do?" I asked.

She reached down, grabbed my hand and pulled me to my feet. "We enjoy the two months we have together. If I remember right, you were going to teach me how to sail."

The End

About Mike Jastrzebski

In September of 2003 my wife, Mary, and I moved aboard our 36-foot sailboat, *Rough Draft*. We sailed the boat from Minnesota to Mobile, Alabama where we lived for two years docked at a small marina. We also spent three months living at a mooring in Key West. Currently, the boat is docked in Ft. Lauderdale, Florida. In 2011 we intend to take the boat to the Caribbean where we plan to drift until it is no longer fun.

When I moved aboard it was my intention that I would write a novel. Six years later I have completed 3 mystery novels. *The Storm Killer, Key Lime Blues (A Wes Darling Mystery), and Dog River Blues* (A Wes Darling Mystery) are all available as trade paperbacks and eBooks.

Contact Mike At: mike@mikejastrzebski.com

Visit Mike's Website: www.mikejastrzebski.com

Visit Mike's Blog: www.writeonthewater.com